A HOUSE WITH WINGS

A Novel

A House with Wings

Library of Congress Cataloging-in-Publication Data
Johnson, Sherrie.
A house with wings / by Sherrie Johnson.
p.   cm.
Summary: Forced from their home for the crime of being Mormon, a girl and
her family experience both danger and the power of forgiveness as they try to
relocate in the Utah Territory.
ISBN 1-56236-309-3
[1. Mormons—Fiction. 2. Frontier and pioneer life—Utah—Fiction. 3.
Utah—Fiction.]   I. Title.
PZ7.J63677Ho   1995
[Fic]—dc20   95-16735
CIP
AC

5 4 3 2 1

Printed in the United States.
Cover painting by Adam Heesch
Art Direction and Design by
Richard Erickson & Rebecca Porter

A HOUSE WITH WINGS

A Novel

Sherrie Johnson

ASPEN BOOKS

$\mathcal{D}$EDICATION

To Ivan E. Cornia
who taught me about "circumstances."

CHAPTER 1

I FIRST SAW DUST PUFFIN' ON THE LAND. I WAS HOEING rows for water, but I stopped to see who it was a comin'. It was a bigger cloud of dust than one horse or even one wagon could make and comin' slow-like from the south. Whoever it was sure wasn't as anxious to be seein' me as I was to be seein' them. I soon noticed that Pa and Aunt Hat were also watchin', Pa restin' on his hoe and Aunt Hat nearby fannin' her face with her apron. As I wiped my face on my skirt, I looked back toward the cabin and sure enough, even my brothers in the field behind had stopped workin'.

Seemed like forever 'fore I could tell it was two wagons comin' along with some horses and a few other animals. I couldn't see the driver of the hind wagon, but the fore wagon was driven by a black man. Didn't take much brains to figure they weren't come visitin'. They were movin' to somewheres. The wagon cover of the front wagon was drawn back revealin' barrels, furniture, trunks and stuff. On the outside chairs, a cradle, tools, buckets, pots, and baskets were roped on till it was most amusin'. But then I could laugh. It wasn't only two years 'fore that we'd done the same thing. Though we didn't have near the belongin's these folks had. The mobbers had seen to that.

As I watched 'em approach, I wished hard as I knew how that they would settle 'long side us, especially if one of 'em was a girl pert near fourteen like me. It'd been a mite lonely out here livin' with five brothers.

Suddenly the wagons stopped and the man on a horse came on alone. Pa walked out to greet him, squintin' like he always does since he doesn't see any too good. "Welcome." Pa took off his hat, wiped at his forehead and over his bald head with his sleeve. Pa put his hat back on, but the stranger didn't remove his, didn't speak. He was lookin' over Pa's head at the rest of us, nervous-like.

"What can I do for ya?" Pa finally asked.

"Ya'll Mormons?" The man asked.

"Yep," Pa said. "And you?"

"No!" The word sounded like a rifle shot.

"We don't see much but our own people and Indians out this way."

"We's on our way to California."

"Trail's back south aways."

"I knows that. My wife's ailin'."

"Should have stopped in Salt Lake City. There isn't much out here and . . ."

"They told us in Salt Lake," the man interrupted, his eyes glarin' at Pa, "there might be some non-Mormons up north. Trappers and a tradin' post or somethin'."

"There'r trappers and a post, but it's no place for a woman, especially if she's sick. You're welcome to stay here if yer so wantin'. My wife has a healin' way about her."

Aunt Hat, who had been listenin' to them talk, stepped forward. "I'd be pleased to look after her."

The man bit down on his lower lip far enough to take a bite of his frazzled brown beard. He didn't want to stay. I could tell that. He looked at my brothers who had walked in from the fields to hear what was goin' on. It wasn't often we got visitors. Matter a fact it was near to never which explains why even Aaron and Brigham were standin' still and starin' out to the spot where the two wagons were stopped.

The sun kept movin', but the man said nothin', just kept on a glarin' at us. I was wonderin' which had the most heat in it, the sun or his eyes, when he finally turned in his saddle and looked back at the wagons while rubbin' at his chin whiskers. Then he looked north. "Them Injuns don't bother ya'll?" he asked, pointin' behind our fields to the village of Indian tepees.

"They're Shoshoni Indians," Pa said. "They keep to themselves mostly. But if it hadn't been for them we wouldn't a made it through the winter."

"There more Injuns goin' north?"

"Yep," Pa answered. "Shoshoni also. The Utes are south a here."

"Injuns is Injuns!" The man took off his hat, revealin' a halo of wet, matted hair, and with his hat off the sun showed up the sweat tricklin' over his cheeks and into his beard. He fidgeted with the hat a spell, then began fannin' his face with it, then he looked hard at Aunt Hat as if considerin'. Aunt Hat, mostly just bone and skin, stared back at first, but then, discomforted, she let her eyes fall to the ground. Land a mighty! I was uncomfortable under that gaze even though he wasn't lookin' at me, but it surprised me a mite that Aunt Hat would be bothered by it. Nothin' bothered Aunt Hat. Why I'd even seen her use an ax to take the head off'n a rattler without so much as battin' an eye.

"What's ailin' yer wife?" Pa asked.

The man stroked at his beard. "Nuttin'," he answered gruffly. "Anyways, it ain't no sickness that's catchin', if it's worryin' ya."

"I wasn't worryin'. Just wonderin'. If yer wife is ailin', she needs help."

"But yer Mormons," he said, each word distinct like he intended much more meanin' behind them than he was sayin'. I'd heard it before, the tone, the anger, and suddenly I realized that without willin' it to do so, my body had tensed so that every muscle was tight and my heart was racin'.

"Doesn't matter." Pa seemed calm enough. But I could see he was gettin' hot and not from the sun. He was holdin' the hoe harder and his knee was jerkin' like when he was mad at me or the boys or like it did the night the mobs ordered us out of Nauvoo. I was only nine then, but I still remember his leg jerkin' same as now.

I don't know if the man saw it, too, but suddenly he yelled, "I'll be back!" and before Pa could answer, he turned his horse and galloped back to the wagons. Pa glanced around as if seein' where Jed and Lije were. (Lije being short for Elijah and Jed for Jedediah) Then just as unsettlin'-like, Aunt Hat mounted Jetty, without even a saddle, and followed the man.

"Hat!" Pa called, but she was gone.

"How am I supposed to raise a passel a children to behave when my own wife don't pay me no mind?" But he was smilin'. He always complained in words about Aunt Hat's spunk, but he never could hide the fact that deep down inside he liked it. That smile calmed me a mite and I took a deep breath. Pa didn't seem worried.

"Jed, Lije, you best fetch some water from the spring. Millennium," he called to me, "into the cabin

and see what Hat's got for 'em to eat. She'll be talkin'
'em into stayin'. The devil himself couldn't refuse that
woman if she asked him to repent."

I smiled, but I didn't like what he was tellin' me to
do. We were just commencin' to have any food at all.
Why durin' the winter my stomach had taken to
growlin' 'long about November and hadn't stopped
since. I'd been eyein' the corn a growin' in the fields
and waitin' for it to ripen. Pa said two more weeks, but
I didn't know if I could wait that long. Now he wanted
us to feed strangers that didn't even like us! But I knew
if I mentioned it Pa would tell me the story of how Jesus
fed the multitudes with only seven loaves of bread and
a few little fishes. So I wasn't about to mention it.

I stood on the wooden trunk and shuffled the
mostly empty baskets that were on the shelf Pa had
attached to the wall. There was some dry corn bread
and some sego lily root. I tried not to think about what
we would be havin' for breakfast, especially if Pa gave
this little bit to the newcomers. The thoughts were too
depressin' so I filled up my head with thoughts of how
fine Aunt Hat's Blue Willow dishes would look on that
shelf, how fine they'd make this dark room look. Well,
maybe not *that* fine. Pa always says I'm one for exag-
geratin'. But those dishes were the only nice thing Aunt
Hat had left. I remember the time I came in and saw the
trunk open—it's never open, mind you—and Aunt Hat
was huggin' on one of the plates. As soon as she saw

me, she put the plate back in the trunk so fast I was sure she'd be breakin' it. I thought I even saw tears in her eyes. But later I reckoned I was mistakin' on that one. Aunt Hat's not one for cryin'. Not Aunt Hat!

That was the only time I've seen those fancy dishes out of the trunk since we left Nauvoo. Aunt Hat worked hard takin' in washin' in addition to her regular school teachin' job in order to buy those dishes, and she says they're the only nice thing she has left in this world and that she's savin' them for some special happenin'. I asked once what kind of special happenin' and she said she wasn't sure, but that it had to be an occasion that would make her think good of men again. I still don't reckon I understand exactly what kind of happenin' she meant, but Aunt Hat isn't one you can ask the same question of twice.

I remember those fine dishes, though. They're covered with fancy pictures from a place Lije called China. I mainly remember the picture of the fancy house, a house that had a roof with wings. Matter a fact, I didn't need to look at a plate to see that house again. I had it in my mind. Why I'd thought on that house a passel a times a day while we were walkin' across the plains. I'd think about livin' in a house with wings when my feet got to hurtin' so bad from walkin' or when my mind got to hurtin' just as bad from thinkin' on what the mobbers had done to us. Seems to me nobody could drive a family out of a house with wings. Land a mighty, no! Why the house could just go with a body even if mobs drove 'em out.

Now at that moment I wasn't hurtin' in my mind or feet, but just standin' atop that trunk where I knew those dishes were hid up made me see that house all over again like some magic was sendin' the vision through the lid a the trunk into the bottom of my feet and up into my eyes. A house with wings! It plumb sent gooseflesh up and down my arms. Why a house with wings could always go where food was, like a bird. No one would ever have to be hungry, and if the neighbors got mean or hated Mormons, the house could just fly away to a new place.

Suddenly the sound of wagons interrupted my dreamin'. I ran to the door to see, but when they reached the creek they turned west and moved away from us. Aunt Hat came on to the cabin.

"They're staying, but they'll make their camp down the creek a ways." By now I was back outside watchin'. They pulled the wagons beside each other and began settin' up camp. I was rememberin' the hundreds of times we'd done it and was thinkin' on how glad I was that it was them and not me doin' it this time, when I saw the girl. She was a distance away, mind you, but she looked to be about my age. There were only three other families this far north of Salt Lake City and none of them had a girl my age. Even if they had they were a good three miles east of us up in Sessions

Settlement. I hadn't had a female person other than Aunt Hat to talk to in the year we'd been here, unless you counted the Indian girl, Tew-yu, and I wasn't sure she counted since we couldn't really talk.

As I watched the girl, I suddenly realized that she was watchin' me too. Not stoppin' and just watchin' like I was, but glancin' my way while she worked. Sure enough she must be wantin' to meet me as much as I was her! I wished hard that she was closer.

"Do they need any help?" I asked.

"I do say, Millennium, you sometimes surprise yer pa. That was a right nice thought, but Hat says they don't want any interferin'. She said they made that very clear."

"What's wrong with the woman?" I asked.

Hat looked at me as if decidin' how to answer, and that was an answer.

"She's a bit discomforted," Hat said.

I smiled. The woman was 'bout to have a baby! You'd think when a person is thirteen and has walked across a whole prairie, driven oxen, beaten clouds of crickets, rocked sick babies through the night, and done a passel a things that other thirteen-year-olds have never thought about, you'd be treated a mite different. But then I might not ever be treated different, least-ways not by Aunt Hat.

"What they want most is to be left alone," Aunt Hat said lookin' direct at me. "He made it clear he doesn't want anyone—do you hear me Millennium?—going near their camp. Now we best stop staring and get back to work."

Slowly I went back to waterin' what should be turnin' into taters, that is if we could keep the critters from eatin' 'em first. But I was still watchin' the strangers as oxen were unharnessed and canvas thrown up for shelter. I was hoein', but my mind was churnin'. Why couldn't the man camp near the side of us? He was a strange one sure. They'd be closer to the spring here, not to mention the outhouse, but most of all they'd be closer to Aunt Hat so she could be carin' for the missus. But I left off wonderin' and began thinkin' on the girl. Every now and again I caught sight of her, and the more I saw the more I wondered on how I was goin' to be meetin' her. Pa or no Pa, somehow I'd figure a way. I had to!

CHAPTER 2

NEXT MORNIN' I WAS OUT 'FORE THE SUN. BUT THAT'S nothin' unusual. Mornin's are the best part of the day and I like greetin' them before they greet me. Smoke was already floatin' from the Indian village. If I squinted my eyes tight, I could make out the women walkin' between the tepees that the Indians lived in. But I wasn't near enough to make out who they were. 'Sides that, I didn't look long. Instead I had my eye on the two wagons camped in the other direction. Aunt Hat said they were a family named Ross and hailed from North Carolina.

I was jealous of Lije and Jed. They slept outside in the wagon bed where they could keep their eyes on the newcomers all night. But Pa says it's not fittin' for me to be sleepin' outdoors. I never could figure why so many things are fittin' for Lije and Jed just because they're boys and older. 'Sides that it was plenty fittin' the past years. It was fittin' then for the whole family. Even after we came here, we slept in the wagon bed under a canvas for a year before we built the cabin. Why we'd only had the cabin a few months. For all I cared we never could have built it. I'd been missin' the sight of the stars and the Indian fires dyin' away at night and the songs of the critters. Sure Pa said you could hear 'em inside, but it wasn't the same song, not when you were hearin' it through logs. But most, I missed the space. It's a mite different sleepin' in the whole wide world than it is sleepin' in that tiny, windowless cabin.

I took the bucket to the spring and filled it full up. The new folks were stirrin'. Aunt Hat had gone down several times to tend to Mrs. Ross. She came back with new parcels of news each time, but there was still a bushelful I was wantin' to know. Aunt Hat said they had a girl named Sarah, but they called her Sary, and she agreed that this Sary must be near to my age. There was one older sister, Suzanna, that I hadn't noticed at all, but from the way Lije blushed when Aunt Hat spoke of her I figured he had. There was also a little brother, Robert, and the black man I'd seen was the Ross's slave boy, George. Aunt Hat was not much on slavery, so that's what she mostly talked on every time she came back from their camp. She'd go on and on about how Mr. Ross ordered the boy about as if he were property, and about how sadness wept from the boy's eyes, and about how it just weren't fittin' for one human being to be treatin' another like that. But then we knew all about how unright human treatment could be.

Now that's what she talked about, but what she wasn't talkin' on was just as interestin'. The second time Aunt Hat went down, she took some herbs she'd brewed into medicine and some food—such as we had—but she brought it all back with her! The food that is. The woman took the medicine fine, Aunt Hat told us all about that. But Aunt Hat put the basket of sego lily roots on our table and only said, "They got better."

All night I dreamed of what that better was. I tried to count up the months since I'd tasted anything good. It was too far back. Why we hadn't even had flour to make Lumpy Dick since April. Not that Lumpy Dick is any treat, just flour stirred into boiling water. Why back in Nauvoo, I never would have touched Lumpy Dick unless it was sugared up. Oh, sugar! I almost don't even remember what that tasted like. But I'm not complainin'. We're blessed to have anythin', what with the crickets feastin' on everything that pushed through the earth that first year. They 'most destroyed everything before the miracle. At least I wasn't starvin', but it had been a long spell since somethin' sat in my mouth to be savored.

It seems strange that just as I was thinkin' that very thought, the unmistakable smell of fryin' bacon met up with my nose. I jerked around so fast I spilled water on my skirt. Jed and Lije must have smelled it too. Jed was just comin' back from the outbuildin' still tyin' up his pants and Lije was in the midst of yokin' the oxen, but now they stopped still as death, all facin' the Ross camp, facin' into the direction of that soft breeze. Even the little ones had stopped their ruckus. The sight of 'em all starin' with their mouths hangin' open set me to laughin'.

I hurried back up to the house with the water. "And what's so amusin'?" Jed asked.

"You. Your tongue's hangin' out like a dog's! And I can hear your stomach growlin' and yer pantin' like a dog, too."

He ignored me, which was a mite unusual for Jed. "Bet they've got real saleratus biscuits to go along with that bacon," Jed said.

"And we got johnnycakes," I said, tryin' not to let on how good just the sound of the word biscuit was to me.

"Johnnycakes are good when you've got the proper fixin's, especially the molasses. But cornmeal mixed with milk don't come near to bein' a johnnycake even if ya call it one. And it ain't as good as real saleratus biscuits," Jed said.

"You let Aunt Hat hear you talkin' like that and you might never eat again!" I whispered as Jed passed me on his way into the cabin.

"She cain't hear from in there!" But I noticed he was whisperin' himself now.

"You two at it again?" Lije asked, and Jed and I both shook our heads at the same time.

Jed and Lije went on into the cabin. Now usually I hated goin' in. Bein' inside that dark, teensy cabin made me feel 'most smothered. But this mornin' I was more than glad to do it because I hoped that being inside I couldn't smell what I'd been smellin'.

I sat on the trunk that became my chair at meal-time and I tried real hard not to think on what the Ross family was eatin', or rather what I wasn't. I tried focusin' on the picture of that house with wings, but my mind was so full up with smells that I couldn't make the picture come. I tried concentratin' on how I was sittin' on the trunk with the dishes in it and hoped that would work. But all it did was make me aware of how hard that seat was.

I figure the others were doin' the same sort of thing, 'cause it was a right quiet breakfast. Matter of fact, no one spoke a word. There was just the sound of dishes knockin'. Even Jacob seemed to know better than to say anything. It wasn't long and Lije stood up to go.

"That family out there doesn't want anyone bother-in' 'em," Pa said before Lije hit the door. "You're not to go near their camp. Hat's the only one Mr. Ross will allow near. I think we best oblige his request."

"Why?" Jed asked.

"I reckon it hangs on us being Mormons."

Jed and Lije's eyes met in that way they had of speakin' eye to eye. They didn't know that I could read it. But I could. They were askin', "Trouble?" When you've been driven out of your home five times in thirteen years you're always fearin' trouble. But surely it couldn't happen now, not with there bein' more Mormons than outsiders around these parts. Surely Mr. Ross wouldn't think that he and George could take on all of us?

"Don't set your minds to worryin'," Pa said as if he read it too. "I don't expect trouble. Hat says the woman is very sick."

"Poor soul wouldn't have made it to the trading post," Aunt Hat knotted up her lips and eyebrows and shook her head in that jerky way she had of doin' things. "I don't know what that man was thinking! It's amazing how hate will distort a man's judgment! Make him so he can't even think straight."

"Hat'll have the woman better soon and they'll be movin' on. For now just stay out of their way."

I could tell that set fine with Jed, but I wasn't so sure about Lije. And me? Well it didn't set well at all. I hadn't seen another girl that I could speak with for over a year, and now I was bein' told I couldn't speak with this one that was right here within hallooin' distance. What was Pa thinkin'? I set my mouth firm, but I didn't say a word.

"Now, Millennium Boxall!" Pa said.

"What?" I tried actin' surprised.

"Mind what I say," Pa looked hard at me. "You're not to go near those folks."

I didn't answer. I knew it was an idea I couldn't put a promise to and so I hoped Pa wouldn't force one from me.

"What do you want me to do when I'm through waterin' the corn?" Jed asked.

It wasn't often I was grateful for Jed, but this time I was. I cleared away my plate and grabbed the bucket.

"I'll fetch the water for dish washin'," I called over my shoulder and was gone.

I don't know what was racin' faster, my mind or my feet. Somehow I had to meet that Sary girl. I was about to the spring when I noticed her carryin' a bucket and movin' in the same direction. My mind took to feelin' smug about how my wishin' had been granted and all so easy-like when Mr. Ross stepped from between their wagons and seein' me already at the spring called Sary back. I couldn't hear his words, but I knew what he was sayin'. I even imagined his eyes were glarin' like they had the day before.

I was more than a mite disappointed, but at that moment my problem also seemed close to solvin'. Maybe Mr. Ross could call Sary back 'cause I was already at the spring, but if she were there and then I came, he couldn't do a thing about it. I'd just watch. Aunt Hat was always needin' water for one thing or another. No one could fault me for fetchin' water.

Hurriedly I filled the bucket and then toted it back to the cabin. Sary started out as soon as I reached the cabin, but I'd wait. Mr. Ross would be watchin' now, and I didn't want her to be gettin' in any kind of trouble.

Inside the cabin, I heated the water over the fire and we washed dishes in silence. Aunt Hat was never one for speakin' much, but this mornin' she seemed farther away than usual. Sometimes I wondered on what it was she thought so hard on, but this mornin' my mind was full up with my own thoughts. It wasn't till we were finished that she finally spoke, "I need you to churn butter this morning."

Usually it was a chore I hated, but today the thoughts of standin' still while poundin' the paddle were more than welcome. I could watch the strangers for a good long spell while churnin'.

"Wish we had two cows," Aunt Hat said, but not like she was sayin' it to me. "This morsel of cream is not going to make much butter."

"It'll do," I answered—even though I knew she wasn't speakin' to me—so as to make sure she didn't do somethin' foolish like change her mind and save the cream for eatin'.

"It'll have to," Aunt Hat sighed. "But there's not enough for the churn. I'll put it in a jar and you can shake it into butter." She poured the cream into a jar and handed it to me. Usually I'd a been a bit upset at that, too. Shaking a jar up and down long enough for cream to become butter wears a body's arm down terrible. But, like I say, I wasn't goin' to argue today.

"You sure are full of help this morning," Aunt Hat said.

I didn't say anything, but I was surprised she'd even noticed. I took the jar outside, leaned against the rough, log wall, and began shakin' that cream. Usually I was aware of the rhythm of slosh and swish, but today I was too busy lookin' south. At some moment Sary would go to the spring, and I had to be watchin' for that moment. But watch as I did nothin' stirred in the Ross camp, leastwise not as I could see.

But I kept on shakin' and watchin' and hardly even noticin' how tired my arms were feelin'. Then about the time I could feel the lumps of butter beginnin' to form, I saw Sary with bucket in hand, headin' for the spring again. My insides went to movin' all about, and I set the jar down and started for my bucket. Then I thought twice. Pa's always tellin' me I need to do that. For once I did. I decided I'd best wait till she was at the spring so Mr. Ross wouldn't call her back again. I waited. Then just as she began to fill her bucket I grabbed mine and set out for the spring at a full trot.

"Millennium," Aunt Hat called, but I didn't look back.

Sary was about finished when I reached the spring. "Howdy," I said.

She looked at me but didn't answer. It felt as if she'd thrown the whole bucket of cold water over me. I'd kept seein' her and wantin' to talk, but the thought that she might not be wantin' to talk back had never crossed my mind afore. Maybe she didn't like me any more than her pa liked Pa.

But in the same instant that I thought that awful thought I pushed it away. It'd been past a year since I'd had another girl to talk to. Somehow I'd make her like me. I had to.

"My name's Millennium. Aunt Hat told me yours is Sary. I know your Pa doesn't want you talkin' to me so you don't need to be talkin'. I'll talk and you listen. I'm sure he didn't give you any instructions about not listenin' so you won't be disobeyin' none. I'm thirteen. I've got five brothers. Two older, three younger. I don't see girls any too often, so I was glad to see you. I know we could be real good friends. I don't know what your pa's told ya, or what he's got against us, but I'm friendly, real friendly." I was talkin' so fast I forgot to look at her, but when I did I wished I hadn't. Her eyes squinted into a questionin' gaze that was far worse than her not talkin', but as soon as my eyes met hers she dropped her head so as not to look at all.

"Sary!" Mr. Ross called from their wagons. "Git on back, ya hear!"

Sary turned. I was desperate. "You'll like me, I know ya will. Meet me behind those tall willows along the creek after noon eatin'," I managed to say as she started back.

She didn't turn or speak. She didn't even act as if she noticed I was there. I shook my head tryin' to escape the feelin' that I'd been struck invisible, and filled the bucket.

I walked slower back to the cabin than I had comin'. Aunt Hat was waitin' for me at the churn. "Your pa told you not to bother those folks!"

"I wasn't botherin' 'em. I'm about finished makin' butter and I knew you'd be needin' water soon."

"I've never had so much water in my entire life! Why you are much more efficient than indoor plumbing," Aunt Hat said. I hated it when she talked all high falutin' like that, usin' big words that nobody understood. Sometimes Jed made fun of her—when she wasn't listenin' that is. He'd pull his body in so he looked near as skinny, and he'd jerk when he moved and use all those big words, and sometimes I'd laugh so as to squeeze water out of my eyes.

"I think it best," Aunt Hat went on, "that you not fetch water anymore unless I tell you to. There are a few things you don't understand, Millennium. If you'll promise to obey, I won't tell your pa this time."

"I promise," I said loud and firm. But even as I said the words I was relishin' the idea that Aunt Hat hadn't said a word about not goin' to the creek.

CHAPTER 3

$\mathcal{I}$T SEEMED AS IF THE SUN WOULD NEVER CLIMB TO THE top of the sky. We washed clothes in the creek, gathered ash for makin' lye which in turn was for makin' soap, boiled dinner, such as it was, and finally Aunt Hat banged the pot callin' everyone to come eat. It wasn't much; sego lily root—again—cattail that the Indians had taught us how to eat, and johnnycakes. I was tired of the mild onion taste of sego lily. For weeks at a time last winter it's all we had. Then the Indians traded us some cornmeal for one of Aunt Hat's quilts. I was mighty grateful for that, but I had learned to be careful eatin' it.

First time we ate it, Jed lost a tooth from bitin' down on a piece of rock. That's why now he crushes his johnnycake and then eats the crumbs. The rocks get in there from the Indian's grindin' stones, so we all learned to eat it slow and careful-like. Least it was food, and now there was even hope a comin' what with the huntin' the boys could do and the corn about to ripen. I shouldn't have had complainin' thoughts, but my head was still full of the bacon smell from the mornin' which caused my stomach to set to growlin' even while it was being filled.

I tried thinkin' on other things—like what was goin' to happen at the creek. I hurried through dinner, washed dishes while Aunt Hat silently mended; then started out the door.

"Millennium, you need to watch Jacob."

Land a mighty! I was back in the cabin faster than buckshot. "What?"

"Where's that helpfulness you've displayed all morning? I've got to tend to Mrs. Ross and I need you to get Jacob to sleep."

"But he never goes to sleep anymore! I'll be in here smotherin' to death for hours! There's not a breath of air in here. I'll die if'n I have to stay in here!"

"Millennium!" I could tell she was about to scold me, but she smoothed her already tight hair tighter to her head and as she did she changed her mind. "All right. Take Jacob for a walk and wear him down a bit."

She was gatherin' up her birthin' bag and the herb tea she'd brewed and didn't seem to notice how that pleased me.

"Come on Jacob," I said. "Let's go pick a big bouquet of sunflowers."

"No," Jacob said, but I expected him to say that, him being two years old and all.

"Maybe Tew-yu will come today," I said even though I knew she wouldn't. She hadn't come since early spring and Lije said she probably wouldn't ever come again. She was a woman now and couldn't play. But Jacob didn't know all that.

Jacob climbed off the chair and waddled out of the cabin. I followed.

"You be careful, hear?" Aunt Hat called. "And don't forget your bonnet."

Aunt Hat always said that but usually also added a discourse on avoidin' freckles which she made out to be the worst curse a female soul could suffer. But this time I wasn't about to argue with her 'bout how I'd never had a freckle before and didn't expect to now. You don't argue with Aunt Hat, especially if there's somethin' you want to be doin'. I grabbed the bonnet off the square nail on the door and in a few steps caught up to Jacob. He wouldn't let me take his hand so I just followed. "Let's play in the willows 'fore we gather the flowers," I suggested. "It's the only place with a mite of shade and you can even wade in the creek a bit."

I was talkin' to Jacob, but my eyes were on the two wagons. I couldn't catch sight of anybody. I looked north to the Indian teepees. Things were quiet there, too. I looked back at the wagons, hopin' now some person, 'specially a Sary person, would be walkin'. But there was no one 'ceptin' Aunt Hat.

Jacob tripped over a rock and started yowlin'. I grabbed him up quick as hot oil and tried not to let Aunt Hat see that I noticed she was stopped and watchin' after me. Jacob quit cryin' when I kissed his knee, and Aunt Hat went on walkin'. Pa, Lije, Jed, Aaron and Brigham were in the fields tryin' to make things grow. They were forever plowin' and waterin'. I still wasn't countin' on it doin' much good, however. As far as my eyes could behold there wasn't even a tree in the valley 'cept the willows that grew along the creek. But there certain sure was plenty of sagebrush, weeds, and sunflowers. A mountain man we'd met when we first came, named Jim Bridger, had called it a desert. He said we couldn't grow a thing here. Pa only laughed when he heard it and said, "Sounds like we've finally found a place no one else'll want! Now that's what I call a blessin'!"

But it didn't look like a blessin' to me. When we ran out of brush for a fire, Pa had to go clear to the mountains for firewood. Then when it came time for buildin', it took him two entire days just to get one wagonload of logs for the cabin. Course we had plenty of rocks for the chimney! But it's a wonder the cabin ever got built what with all the haulin' it took!

Jacob and I reached the willows, parted the branches and wandered in, savorin' the cool that washed over us in delicious breaths. I'd once read about a jungle and wondered if this was anything near what a jungle felt like. Jacob headed right into the water 'fore I could roll his pant legs up. His bare feet splashed and he giggled. I kept one eye on Jacob and the other on the wagons. Not a soul was stirrin'.

I swallowed hard and tried not to feel the misery that came swarmin' into my chest. It just wasn't fair. I'd been livin' with only brothers for over a year. I'd scarce laid eyes upon another girl, and now there was one right aside me and her pa wouldn't let her talk with me. She had to come. She just had to. Still nothin' moved except Jacob. I sat down on the creek bank and waited. Hope seemed a distant enough fellow, but I still couldn't let go of it.

Suddenly Jacob fell. He screamed and I jumped in to pick him up before he breathed water. Bein' early July, there wasn't much water, mind you, but it only took an inch to drown a child. Pa was always sayin' that.

The fall had feared Jacob and he kept screamin'. I grabbed him up and wiped the water off his face with my skirt. Then I hugged him till his sobbin' died out and glanced to see if Aunt Hat was comin'. There was no sign of Aunt Hat, but I thought I caught sight of Sary crossin' from the wagons to the creek. Not in my direction mind you, but straight out from the wagons to the creek nearest her. I held my breath, almost forgettin'

about Jacob. But he tugged on my bonnet strings, pullin' my face to his so we were nose to nose.

"I's hurt, Milly," he said. I looked down and saw his knee was bleedin'. Must have cut it on a rock. I dipped my patched skirt in the creek and wiped his knee off. It wasn't much of a cut and the trickle of blood soon stopped, but Jacob wouldn't quit whimperin'.

"It's all right," I kept sayin', but I was lookin' off down creek tryin' to figure whether Sary was comin' or not. I'd pointed this place out this mornin'. She couldn't have mistook it. It's the place where the willows grow highest. I waited. Jacob stopped cryin' and wiggled out of my arms. My patched dress was soaked from holdin' his wet body, but it added to the cool. I was lookin' for a move in the willows or a catch of Sary's unpatched brown dress. But the way the creek meandered, I couldn't see even if she *was* comin'. Then I heard her. She was walkin' in the water. I scurried down the bank and was starin' full on when she appeared.

"Howdy!" I said and she stopped. "I knew you'd come. You just *had* to come. I've been waitin'."

Sary looked back toward the wagons worried-like. She pushed her straight, brown hair off her forehead into her bonnet, but even with the bonnet I could see that her hair was so thick that if it was braided up, the braid would begin the size of my fist! Slowly she looked back to me.

"I didn't believe ya when ya said yer name was Millennium, but yer ma said it's the truth," she spoke with words so full of the South that they almost startled me, though I don't know why it should have, seein' that her pa had spoken the same. She was fidgetin' with her hair and scratchin' at her leg with her foot and drummin' her fingers that weren't in her hair on her leg so that she seemed all motion even though she wasn't goin' anywhere.

"She's not my ma," I said. "My mother died birthin' my only sister when I was four years old. The baby died too. A while later my Pa married my ma's sister so Hat's my aunt. Jacob here is hers and Pa's, but I'm only Pa's."

She was still facin' me, and I suddenly had a thought of men preparin' for a gunfight. I started to smile, almost laughed, but then worried on how Sary would feel about me burstin' into laughter. It's a good thing I stopped myself. Once I had my senses again, I noticed that Sary's face had gone whiter than snow. She wasn't sayin' a word, just starin' at me. Wasn't even fidgetin'.

"She's dead 'cause of birthin'?" Sary asked, and then I knew what the problem was.

"Yes, but Aunt Hat wasn't her midwife. I wish she had a been, but she wasn't there when the baby started comin'. Aunt Hat never loses a mother. I heard Pa say that lots of times. Matter of fact he's always braggin' on

it. Makes him right proud that fact does." I knew I was
"rattlin'" as Aunt Hat often told me, but I didn't know
what else to do but rattle. "Aunt Hat will take fine care
of your ma. You'll see. Fine care. She always does."

Sary looked back again at the wagons, her green
eyes fidgitin' almost as much as her body had. I thought
for a moment she might turn and run, but she didn't.
Instead she sat herself down on the bank, leavin' her
feet in the water. "Pa would skin me good if'n he knew
I was talkin' to ya'll."

"I won't tell," I said. "That's for sure!"

"Well, I knowed that," Sary said, and a light came
into her green eyes chasin' away the feared look she'd
been wearin' there. "And he cain't fault me for wadin'
on a hot day like this. I've never disobeyed Pa before. I
seen what he does to George when he doesn't do something the way Pa wants it done. You don't cross Pa,
that's a truth."

"I told you I won't tell," I said.

"I knowed that or I wouldn't have come, but it
sure enough feels strange to do somethin' I'm wantin'
to do when Pa's said no."

"Is George the black man?" I asked.

"Sure is. Only he ain't really a man yet. Sixteen
years old. Pa owned his pa and ma, but he sold them
when we come west. Said he couldn't feed three of
'em."

"Sold his pa and ma!" I'd heard all about the

terrors of slavery, but somehow the thought of a child havin' his parents sold away from him had never occurred to me.

"You one of those abolitionists or somethin'?" The tone of Sary's voice told me I'd better be talkin' of somethin' else if I didn't want her runnin' away. Pa would be proud of me—he says I usually say anythin' I think up without ever considerin' how it'll ring to others. But this time I did some considerin' and that caused me to be changin' the subject.

"Aunt Hat says you're from North Carolina."

Sary's eyes were still squinty and her face tight. She pulled at the hair that hung from under her bonnet, wiggled her feet in the water, stared for a minute as if thinkin' hard and then said, "I was borned there."

The word *born* made me think of children. That made me think of Jacob and how quiet things had become. I looked up the creek. He wasn't there.

"Jacob?" I cried. "Land a mighty! I forgot I was tendin' to Jacob."

I jumped and ran up the middle of the shallow creek. Sary followed. At first I was so filled with fear that I lost my head. "Easy now," I told myself and took in a deep breath of hot air. That's how I always got my head on again. Then I retraced the steps I'd been runnin'. This time I watched the bank careful-like. Sure enough there was a wet place where Jacob had climbed out of the water.

"There's where he went," I showed Sary. "Wait here. I'll fetch him back." For a ways I could follow the wet footprints, but then they dried away. Thank goodness he'd climbed out on the far side of the creek so Aunt Hat wouldn't be seein' him or me. "Jacob? Jacob?" I called, but he didn't answer. I was runnin' now and my heart poundin'. Four years of livin' on prairies and seein' and hearin' the tales of all the bad that could happen to a body, especially a little body, sent my heart to boltin' inside my ribs. Why there were wolves and rattlesnakes and all manner of things out in those fields. Not to mention passin' Indians that loved little blond haired boys and girls.

But then I saw his head bobbin' between sunflowers. "Jacob!" I cried. "Jacob!"

He turned and watched me comin'. "Here me is," he said as I gathered him up in my arms.

"What you doin' scarin' a body to death," I cried. "You stay close to Milly!"

Jacob put his arms around my neck and cuddled in. He was almost dry now and he hugged me tight and kissed my neck. There wasn't much I could say then! It's more than a mite hard to be mad at someone who's huggin' at ya like that.

I hurried back to where I'd left Sary and looked around, but she was gone. My ribs filled so with the disappointment that it swelled up into my eyes, causin' a hurt that in another body would have made tears, but

I never cry. I waded down the creek to see if she was there, but she wasn't. Then I saw through the willows, toward the wagons, she was walkin' from the creek where she'd entered. But why'd she leave? She was movin' toward her pa, who was standin' stiff-like and waitin'. Had he found her out? Maybe he'd called her back. But Sary was skippin', joyful-like. I hoped hard that she wasn't headed for a passel of trouble and hoped even harder that she hadn't left on account of not likin' me. All that talk of dyin' while birthin'! And slavery! Why didn't I think? Surely there was somethin' we could have talked about that both of us could think the same on.

Slowly I walked back to the cabin. Jacob, heavy in my arms, fell asleep. That part was right fine. Aunt Hat would be pleased. But I couldn't stop thinkin' on Sary. I hadn't had a chance to arrange another meetin', and there was so much more I was needin' to ask her. Sary and her pa disappeared between the wagons, and I took Jacob in and set him on a pallet on the floor. My plan halfway worked, but now I needed one that all the way worked. But what was it goin' to be?

CHAPTER 4

$\mathcal{T}$HE NEXT DAY, I SAT BACK AGAINST THE WALL, LISTENIN' to Jacob breathin' during his noontime nap and wonderin' on a plan. But my mind wouldn't stay with thinkin' things up. Sittin' there in the dark other thoughts kept creepin' into me. I tried pushin' 'em away, just as I always did, but just as always it didn't work.

"Exterminatin' order! Exterminatin' order!" The words kept rolling through my mind like thunder that I couldn't make stop. I remembered when I first heard 'em, when I was three. Then, all I knew was that when I heard anyone say them, the words were choked with hate or fearful feelings dependin' on who was sayin' 'em. Now I knew what they meant. Now I knew more than I wanted about exterminatin' orders and fearin' and hatin'.

I tried pushin' away the thoughts! I stared at the outline of light that shone through the cracks in the door and hummed a tune. I even concentrated on how hot and stuffy it was in the cabin. I listened again to Jacob breathin'. But none of it did any good. Talkin' with Sary about my ma had brought too much back into my mind.

Suddenly I was three again and livin' in Missouri and it was a cold February night. I could see Pa stirrin' at the fire, Lije reading at the table, and I could almost feel myself snuggled on Ma's lap. I tried to stop the thoughts right there, tried to remember how it felt with her arms around me and what she looked like when she was peaceful there, but it wasn't any use. Always I tried to stop the picture in that same place, and always the rememberin' kept on goin' even though I didn't want it to.

Suddenly there were horses all around the house, thunderin' around and around and around. Men were shoutin'. Guns firin'. Torchlight flickered through the widows. Pa was callin' things for us to do, but Ma sat frozen as if she couldn't hear him.

The thunderin' sound stopped, but the pawin', whinyin', clangin' noises still rattled outside. "Boxall! Boxall!" a voice outside shouted, "We're here to escort you out of Missouri. If you go peaceful now, there won't be no trouble."

Pa went to the door and opened it slowly. The

sounds grew louder. I buried my head in Ma's chest and closed my eyes tight-like. But it didn't help any. I could hear Ma's heart thumpin' so fast it felt as if it was comin' right through her bones to beat against me. I was holdin' my doll then—holdin' to her tight.

"Please can't you give us a week to pack up? My wife's goin' to have a child and she can't leave without any preparation," Pa begged.

"Governor Boggs ordered you Mormons driven out or exterminated. Since we're God fearin' men we'll drive ya out rather than kill ya, if'n like I said, you'll go peaceful and quick-like. We don't want no trouble."

"Just three days!" Pa said. "I promise I'll go peaceful. Just give me some time."

"Now's as good a time as any!" another voice was almost drowned out by shouts and jeers. I snuggled tighter against Ma, but with her heart beating me that-away it didn't give me any comfort.

"Please! Just a day?" Pa cried.

That's when the guns began firin'. Guns blasted and the men, their faces painted black with gun powder, shouted and commenced threatenin'.

Pa came back inside. He grabbed a quilt off the bed and yelled to the boys. Ma set me down and began shoving things into a bag. The next thing I knew we were outside in that cold, the wind blowing my ears to ice and us runnin'. Guns blasted behind us, dirt sprayed beside us as the bullets hit, but the worst sound of all was the sound of the men laughin' as they shot at us.

Laughin'! The drunken sounds in my mind grew louder! Laughin'! I held my ears to keep out the sound, but since it was comin' from memory instead of from the air it didn't do any good. The sound got louder and the bullets kept coming and we kept runnin' and the cold kept bitin' and all night we ran. We ran until there was no more laughin' and no more firin'. We ran until Ma fell again and this time couldn't get up, and then we huddled beside an old, fallen tree waitin' for morning. And it was cold. So cold. I wanted my doll, but I'd dropped it someplace along the way. It was the doll my grandmother had made me. I took to cryin' and Pa kept tryin' to comfort me, sayin' they'd make me another. But Ma didn't say anything. She just sat in the cold. Staring back to where we'd come from.

Suddenly the door opened and Aunt Hat stepped into the cabin. Relief flooded through me. I wasn't in Missouri. I was in the cabin and it was July not February and I was thirteen not three.

At first Aunt Hat didn't see me sittin' on the dirt floor with Jacob. I heard her sigh as she put her bag on the table. Then she pulled off her bonnet without untyin' it and hung it on the peg from the strings.

I sat there in the dark wonderin' if that's how Ma would have hung her bonnet, them bein' sisters and all. I tried searchin' into the deep places of my brain for some kind of memory, but nothin' came except Ma's face pinched tight like she was hurtin' or somethin'. That was the memory of her that kept comin', even when I didn't want it to. I kept hopin' to see her smilin' or, even better, laughin' or at least hangin' a bonnet or doin' somethin' ordinary-like, but all I ever saw was the face frozen in that hurtin' look. Did she ever hang a bonnet? Did she move in jerks like Aunt Hat? Did she ever smile? Did she sing? Somehow I thought I had a memory of her singin', but every time I tried bringin' it up it faded so I wasn't sure if it was a memory or somethin' I was wantin' to be a memory. Aunt Hat didn't sing much. Was Ma as tall as Aunt Hat? Did she like sunsets and flowers much as I did? I had a million questions about Ma and not many answers. Once I'd asked Pa if Ma was like Aunt Hat, and he told me they weren't much alike, except they were both cultured, but he never did tell me what cultured was or what was the differences between 'em.

"How's Mrs. Ross?" I finally asked, hopin' that by speakin', Ma's pain-filled face would go out of my mind.

Aunt Hat jumped. "Millennium Boxall, you near caused my death."

I laughed. "Wasn't meanin' to. You told me to put Jacob to sleep. He's sleepin' sound."

"Thank-you, Millennium."

Then Aunt Hat did somethin' I don't reckon I'd ever seen her do before. She pulled the bench against the wall near to me, sat down, leaned back against the wall relaxin', and began talkin' just to me.

"You sure are growing up, Millennium. I was surprised this morning to notice that you are near to being a woman! I've been too busy to see it before. And you are looking more like your mother every day. For a minute this morning, when you were bringing in water, I almost thought it was Phoebe. It startled me. I can see her in you. Of course I always have, but it's getting more now. Why the way you just scared me so . . . your ma used to take a great delight in doing that to me when she was about the age you are now."

"No one's ever told me much about Ma."

Aunt Hat looked at me as if puzzled, started to open her mouth and then stopped. It was a minute before she went on, "Why I guess that's so," she said softly. "At first I couldn't talk about her. The hurt stayed on for a long time. Then with crossing prairies and trying to find enough food to stay alive— there are a lot of things that should have been talked about or done that we haven't. She was a wonderful sister, your ma, and you should know all about her. I'll not be so neglectful in the future. I'll think of some things to tell you. Would you like that?"

I wanted to ask her right then to tell me more, but at the same time this sudden talkin' about Ma after never talkin' about her made a feelin' swell into me than I couldn't explain. It was bewilderin'. Finally someone else was talkin' about Ma and I couldn't. Instead I asked Aunt Hat, "Is Mr. Ross mean?"

"No, Millennium," Aunt Hat said slow-like, as if thinkin' about it real hard. "He's a stern man and stubborn, very stubborn, but he's not mean."

"Then why'd he sell George's ma and pa?

It was only as Aunt Hat squinted up her eyes and commenced starin' at me that I realized what I'd done. "How did you come to know that?"

"I must have made a good guess," but I didn't say it at all right. It came out soft and doughy and more like a question than an answer.

"Millennium Boxall?"

There was nothin' to do but tell her the whole story, about Sary that is. I did manage to leave out the parts about Jacob fallin' into the creek and gettin' lost. As I finished, I was expectin' to be punished, but to my surprise Aunt Hat began to chuckle. "Yours hasn't been a normal life, Millennium. How I wish you'd played with dolls and sewed samplers in a parlor with curtains hanging pretty at the window and had all the good books you wanted to read and all the time in the world to read them. But that's not how it is, is it?"

She sat a moment in the dark without saying anything. I watched her long fingers rubbin' at each other and wondered if that's how growin' up had been for her and Ma. Pa said they'd lived in Boston and that they had money and fine things, but they gave it all up to join the Mormon church and go west. But I'd never stopped to think about how fine Pa meant when he said fine things. Lots of books and time for readin'! Land a mighty, that did sound fine.

Finally Aunt Hat went on, and even though she was speakin' to me she was usin' that voice she had when she was talkin' to herself. "Sary needs a friend as much as you do. There's been enough hatin', that's for sure. Now mind you if your Pa asks, I'll have to tell him what I know. But I don't suppose he'll ask, so we can keep this our secret."

Aunt Hat reached out and put a hand on my shoulder. "Just be careful," she said, pattin' me in the same snappy like way she did everythin'.

I was gettin' really brave now. Talkin' like this was different from talkin' while we cooked or washed or worked the soil. It felt good. "You still haven't told me why Mr. Ross sold George's ma and pa. Sary said George is sixteen. That's like someone sellin' Pa away from Jed!"

Aunt Hat had that faraway stare on her face, the

one she gets when she's lookin' at things, but not really seein' 'em. "Mr. Ross is just a man caught in time and doesn't know he's a prisoner."

"What? Mr. Ross is a prisoner?"

Aunt Hat's eyes came back to seein', "No! Certainly not like that. Now what have I said? How do I explain it? It's that he's just doing what his ma and pa and others around him have done for years before him and he's never stopped to reckon whether it's right or wrong or how it hurts another body."

There was a long silence, not countin' Jacob snorin'. "Were there people like that in the mobs that drove us out of Nauvoo?" I asked.

"Reckon so. Of course the ones leading the trouble were stoked up with hate and knew what they were about. But there were others who just heard a fiery speech, got some of that fire in their own souls, and commenced to shouting and shooting!"

I remembered walkin' barefoot and followin' the trail of blood left on the white snow from other folks' feet. I never would look back to see the red my feet were leavin' behind, just kept my eyes forward. Even now I tried not to think about it. At the time I asked Pa why the men were drivin' us out of our home. He only patted my shoulder and said that some folks are so full up with fear they don't have much room inside them for thinkin'. I didn't understand it then, but I suddenly realized that's what Aunt Hat was explainin' now.

My thoughts were interrupted by footsteps and poundin' outside, "Mrs. Boxall, Mrs. Boxall!"

Aunt Hat jumped up and went to the door. Sary entered as she opened it. "Mrs. Boxall, somethin's awful wrong. Pa said to fetch you quick."

Aunt Hat grabbed her birthin' bag and ran. She didn't even take her bonnet. Sary leaned against the door and then fell to the floor and commenced cryin'. "It'll be all right," I said.

Sary looked up, startled. Comin' in from the sun, she must not have seen me. I crawled over beside her and sat on the hard dirt floor.

"Your Ma died birthin'," she said.

"I told you, she didn't have Aunt Hat for a midwife. Besides, Ma didn't die just 'cause of the birthin'."

"Then what was it?"

"We're Mormons and . . ."

"Pa says Mormons are troublemakers."

"We are not! But that's the problem." I tried to keep the anger out of my voice, seein' she was already distressed, but I wasn't succeedin' any too well. "It's folks like your pa that go about sayin' such things! That's why my ma died." I took a deep breath and tried to swallow down some of the anger.

"It wasn't birthin', it was the runnin' from the mobbers in Missouri. It took us weeks to get to Illinois and it was cold and we had no food and . . ."

I had to wait a minute to swallow down the terrible swellin' behind my eyes. I could see that Sary had stopped cryin' and was starin' wide, almost as if she was experiencin' the fear. Again I thought of stoppin', wanted to be stoppin' especially when I saw those eyes, but all at the same time somethin' kept pushin' the words right out of me.

"It was the runnin' and hunger and cold. When it came time for the birthin' she was too weak. She died and the baby too. But Lije said she died 'cause of the hate of the mobbers not 'cause of the birthin'.'"

Sary stared hard for a long spell. Then so fast I barely knew what had happened, she jumped up and was gone. I'd done it again! Talkin' without thinkin'! But every word was true and it felt good sayin' it. But what if it meant I wouldn't have Sary for a friend? I tried to tell myself she'd only be near a few weeks anyway, besides that, I'd messed up so many times already what with always sayin' the wrong thing, that one more sure wouldn't matter much. But it didn't help. When a body has been lonely for over a year, even a few weeks with a friend matters!

The swellin' welled up behind my eyes again and that made me mad. I'd walked clean across the prairie and never shed a tear! Why was I waterin' up now? I sniffed back the water so it couldn't come out of my eyes and shifted my thoughts to somethin' that didn't make tears. It was hard findin' somethin' but finally my mind settled on the field east of the cabin. It took a mite a power, but I got the picture and kept it. I filled my mind so full of yellow flowers and green gangly stems that grow out and up and over as if they can't make up their mind that I could even smell the pungent odor of sunflowers.

"It'll be all right," I whispered back to Jacob's snorin'. "If sunflowers can grow in this place, there is hope! There's got to be! Isn't there?"

CHAPTER 5

I WASN'T TALKIN' ALL THAT LOUD, SO IT MUST HAVE BEEN all the other commotion. Whatever it was, Jacob rolled sudden-like and started whimperin' half in his sleep and half out. As I gathered him up, he cuddled against me, huggin' me tight and then relaxin' into my arms so trustin'-like that it near melted my heart. I kissed his sweatin' forehead and hugged him back and felt the warmth of the hug pass through my skin and muscles and bones and settle with a flutter into my heart. Yep, there was hope, I decided, but I couldn't think on it more. Suddenly the sound of horses and wagon took up my full attention.

Still holdin' to Jacob I stepped outside, but as soon as the sun hit him, he wiggled so I put him down. Pa and the boys were runnin' in from the field. Mr. Ross was drivin' the wagon with one hand, but at the same time he was turned back so that the other arm and his head was almost inside the wagon. It made a strange sight seein' the back of someone's head comin' at me when I was expectin' eyes.

Back at the Ross camp Sary, her sister, brother, and George stood like trees, just starin' at us, a slight breeze flutterin' their skirts and shirts. They were the only thing that didn't seem a mess of confusion standin' still like that.

Aunt Hat caught up to the wagon, then walkin' 'long side she began shoutin' orders. "Pull up in front of the cabin. Mr. Boxall will help you carry her in. It's about time she was near enough so I can tend to her proper! Millennium, pull the covers down."

Mr. Ross did exactly as she said. I grabbed Jacob out of the way of the horses, ran inside, did as I was told, and ran back out still pullin' Jacob along. Pa reached us then.

"Gentle! She needs to be carried gentle-like," Aunt Hat called as the men began liftin' her blankets and all from the wagon bed. Aunt Hat called after them, "Easy. Put her on the bed."

As they passed by me I was startled to see that Mrs. Ross's face was pale as moonlight and her thick brown hair, just like Sary's, spilled over the blanket and onto her shoulders in tangles and twists. She was on her back and the swollen mound under the blankets seemed a mite out of place what with everything else lookin' so depleted.

"Brigham, take Jacob," Aunt Hat continued shoutin' orders. "Millennium, go get Sary to help and ask George and Suzanna to bring the other wagon up close so they can camp near."

I looked at Mr. Ross expectin' him to be arguin', but he wasn't seein' or hearin' anythin' but his wife.

I took off runnin', my insides poppin' and feelin' frizzy—as if someone had poured gunpowder into my blood and then set it afire. When Sary saw me comin', she started toward me and as she drew near I could see that her face was near as pale as her ma's and her eyes had a numb look about them. The others followed her. "Aunt Hat needs us," I said soon as she was near enough. "And she wants Suzanna and George to bring the other wagon up and camp so you'll be near." George, Suzanna, and Robert started back. I turned then and started runnin' back toward the cabin. Sary soon caught up to me. Pa and Mr. Ross were standin' outside now. Mr. Ross was pacin' like a wild animal that's boxed in and Pa was standin' helpless, not knowin' what to do with his arms or what words to be sayin'.

Aunt Hat poked her head out the door. "There is nothing you can do here now. Go on back to work. I've got her where I can care for her, and she's much more comfortable. Now go on! You'll only worry her standing around like this."

Mr. Ross kicked at the dirt sendin' up a cloud of

dust. "This settin' round ain't natural fer a man. Give me a plow!"

Pa looked startled. I knew that was the last thing he was expectin' from Mr. Ross. "Sure," he said, "another hand would be welcome, but I can't afford payin' ya."

"I ain't said nuthin' 'bout pay," Mr. Ross growled. "Jist keep me busy."

"I can do that," Pa said and started for the field. Lije and Jed followed, but Aaron and Brigham hung back reluctant like. "I still need you two," Pa called without even lookin' back. There are times I swear Pa has eyes all around his head.

"Millennium, I need more of that water you've taken such delight in fetching. Sary, you help her."

I'm still not sure, but I almost thought I saw Aunt Hat wink at me as she said that. With all the commotion, I'd clean forgot about my hot words and Sary runnin' off and all. Now I was rememberin' and wonderin' if she was rememberin' too.

Aunt Hat disappeared inside. Worried by all the commotion, Jacob clung to her skirt, makin' me worry that I'd have to be takin' him. But she didn't ask me to.

I grabbed a bucket and handed Sary another. "Nice day," I said and then realized how silly that sounded.

Sary didn't say anything.

"Everything's goin' to be fine now. Aunt Hat can take even better care of yer ma now."

I waited, but still Sary didn't speak.

"I'm sorry for speakin' my mind so," I finally said. "But it was all the truth and there was no reason for ya to run off. Why'd ya go off like that anyway?"

"Cain't speak of it," Sary said firmly while twistin' a strand of that thick brown hair around her finger.

"Land a mighty, Sary! What kind of answer is that?" I said.

"Cain't speak of it," she said even firmer—like the girls in school used to reply when they were doin' sums for the teacher and were certain sure of the answer.

I was a mite annoyed, but I wasn't about to have her runnin' off again. "That's fine," I said as we started for the spring. "We won't speak on it. We'll forget about it. Pretend it never happened. We'll talk about somethin' else." I looked around wonderin' what that somethin' else could possibly be. My mind was so churnin' with what we'd been talkin' on that I figured I'd never come up with another thing, but as I looked up I saw the teepees. "Like the Indians," I said with a smile. "There's a girl lives there just our age. I've met her a few times. She can't speak English. Once last summer we gathered sunflowers and wove them into crowns. But she married Degonda this spring, and I haven't seen her this summer a'tall. She's a woman now. Lije said she was the envy of all the other Indian girls 'cause

Degonda chose her for his bride. Degonda's very brave and very handsome. Anyway that's what Lije says."

"You know her? A real Indian girl?"

"Sure do," I said, encouraged by Sary's interest.

"Aren't you afraid?"

"Nope. Just after we built the cabin we took a trip into Salt Lake City for supplies. Pa let us all go so we left everythin' here unattended to. It took a few days 'cause we stayed on to visit kin. When we came back, the Indians had taken everythin' they wanted. Pa just walked over and talked to 'em. 'Fore long we had 'most everythin' back. Seems they thought we'd left it for 'em. Soon as Pa made it known we'd only gone visitin' they gave it back. Pa says it's a matter of customs and us understandin' theirs and them understandin' ours. He says that understandin' takes time and that you can't fault a fellow for making mistakes along the way to understandin'."

"Ya'll sure do talk on a spell, Millennium Boxall," Sary said.

I wasn't sure that was a kind remark but decided to take it as one. I'd listened close when Pa explained it that day. I felt that Pa must be the wisest man in the entire world what with him havin' such fancy thoughts. Now sayin' it to Sary, I felt a mite fancy myself, and I wasn't goin' to let her ruin the feelin'.

Sary wasn't sayin' anything. Her bucket banged against her leg and her bare feet slapped against the dirt makin' a kind of music. She pulled at her hair and kept bitin' on her lip as if she wanted to be talkin' but was stoppin' herself. I watched, wishin' my hair were straight like that and not so curly like mine is. And that chestnut color! It was beautiful, especially with the sun glistenin' in it. It reminded me of a horse we once had, such a deep, rich brown. My hair besides bein' unmanageable curly wasn't really even a color. Not brown, not blond, but somewhere in between. Jed's always teasin' me that my hair's the same color as used dishwater. *He* should talk. He lost his hat crossin' the plains and has never got a new one. Out in the sun all the time his hair is the color of corn silk. Why God would waste that beautiful color on Jed when I, the only girl in the family, would have appreciated it so, I'll never understand. But there was no use frettin' it. There wasn't much I could do about it even if I did fret.

"Seems as if no one's goin' to object to our speakin' now," I finally said.

"Seems so, though I'm still not sure about Pa."

We filled the buckets in silence. When they were near full Sary said, "Think we could meet your Indian friend?"

"Her name's Tew-yu."

"Tew-yu then. Think we could meet up with her? I's seen braves along the trail and tribes from a distance, but I's never met up with a real Indian girl near to my own age and I's never spoke to one."

"If Aunt Hat can spare us a spell, we can meet her. Course, like I was sayin', she's a wife now and hasn't come to the fields since she up and married. It might be difficult."

By now we were headin' back. George had just hitched up the other wagon and started drivin' to the cabin. It was then that the thought hit me like lightnin' out of the sky. If Mrs. Ross was now sleepin' on the only bed, Pa and Aunt Hat would take the pallet on the floor and I'd be back out in the wagon bed!

For just a twinklin', I felt bad that I was feelin' so good about Mrs. Ross feelin' so bad. But it didn't last long. Why, what with Mrs. Ross ailin', Aunt Hat might even make us take our meals outside! It was as if in one swoop all my problems had just washed away. But then the last time I'd had that feelin' was when Pa made me the wooden doll. He carved it a long while after we'd settled in Nauvoo. He said it was to replace the one I'd left in Missouri. Aunt Hat had sewed a cloth body to attach to the legs and arms and head Pa carved. It was almost life-size and so pretty. I loved her 'most as much as I do Jacob. Course I was only ten then. But the next year, Pa loaded the wagon and we left Nauvoo in such a hurry that I left the doll out by the spring-house. But that much bad couldn't happen three times, could it? Besides that I didn't have a doll now. I was too old for dolls. Why it was just a matter of a few years and I'd have children of my own. But I'd never thought

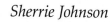

on that and besides it sent so many questions runnin'
through me—like who would I ever find to marry out
here?—that I changed my thoughts back to the present.
If things are goin' good there's no use thinkin' up bad.
Life sends enough bad on its own without me thinkin'
of more!

CHAPTER 6

I WAS SURE ENOUGH RIGHT ABOUT SLEEPIN' IN THE wagon! Come time to bed down, Aunt Hat gave me a quilt and told me to put the canvas on the wagon bed and sleep there. I was so excited I pert near split out of my skin. I didn't even argue with her about the canvas. I figured I could put it halfway up and keep the side that faces the village open. After all she didn't say I had to have the whole canvas on. There was one hitch, however. Besides givin' me a quilt, Aunt Hat gave me Jacob. She didn't want him disturbin' Mrs. Ross durin' the night. But I could manage that fine. I figured I could get Jacob to sleep first and then have time to ponder on the night before I went to sleep.

Lije and Jed took Brigham and Aaron and moved their bedrolls out of the wagon to let me in. They gathered a pile of weeds to sleep on and seemed as excited about that as I did about havin' my outdoors back.

Aunt Hat had invited the Rosses to join us for dinner. I thought that was a right funny offer seein' as how their dinners were a far cry better than anythin' we had to be eatin'. I wasn't a'tall surprised when Mr. Ross declined. I watched as Sary and Suzanna fixed stew with real taters and carrots and salt pork. But the worst was the wheat flour biscuits. My mouth took to waterin' at the smell. Lije watched too. Only I'm not sure his mouth was waterin' only 'cause of the stew. He stopped watchin' when Jed started sayin' about how purty Suzanna was and teasin' him about watchin' her.

I was right about somethin' else, too. Aunt Hat wouldn't even let us inside to eat. She made Jed build a fire outside and brought out the food to cook. Most folks did that lots in the summer to keep from heatin' up the cabin, but Aunt Hat usually insisted on cookin' and eatin' inside so as we'd have some 'semblance of civility. Those were the very words she used! Anyways I didn't care now. We sat against the cabin or wherever we could find a place to be sittin' and ate, and I didn't feel crowded or smothered a'tall. Jed had shot a rabbit that was eatin' on our crops, so we were feastin' good today.

Mr. Ross dished up a bowl of their stew and brought it over for his wife. As he passed me sittin' there with my johnnycake and rabbit he stopped and looked. "The vittles good?" he asked.

"The rabbit's a mite tough, but it's meat," Jed said. "The young bobtails make better eatin'."

"Least it's not squirrel," I said. "I've never taken much likin' to squirrel meat."

"The Indians eat rats and mice," Jed said.

"Don't think I'd take to that, but squirrel ain't bad. Don't ya'll got taters or carrots?" Mr. Ross asked. "How about wheat flour?"

"We're still learnin' to work this land," Lije defended 'fore I could answer. "Our first year here we had a fine early spring and planted what seed we'd brought. Then come the first part of June, thick black blankets of crickets swarmed down from those mountains and commenced eatin' everythin' in their way. For two weeks we tried beatin' 'em, burnin' 'em, buryin' 'em . . ."

"We even dug trenches," Jed interrupted Lije, "and let the water from the creek into the trenches and then drove the crickets into the trenches so as to drown 'em. But as soon as we'd kill one cricket, two more would show up for his funeral. Lost most the crop before it scarce found its way out of the ground."

"How'd ya'll finally whup 'em?"

Jed looked at Pa and Pa nodded. "The problem was bigger than us. We prayed and asked for help from higher up. It weren't long after that great white clouds appeared in the sky. Some feared it was more trouble, but it was the most amazin' thing. When the clouds drew near we could see they were gulls. Thousands of 'em! They landed in the fields and commenced eatin' those crickets fast as they could."

Rememberin' was gettin' Pa all excited and he took over the story tellin'. "If I hadn't seen it with my own eyes I wouldn't have believed it. Those birds would eat and eat and then fly to a stream or creek, drink, and then vomit all they'd eaten. Then they'd fly back where they'd been and commence eatin' more! Around here it's spoken of as the Miracle of '48. Those crickets 'most wiped us out, but we made it. Things have been scarce since. The Indians showed us how to eat sego lilies and thistles and cattails. It's kept us alive. Harvest is startin' now. This year's crop is goin' to be fine. I'll have enough for next year's seed and to get us through the winter. Come fall we'll be eatin' fine."

Mr. Ross shook his head and walked into the cabin with the bowl of stew. When he came back out, he walked over to his stew pot hangin' over the fire, lifted it off with a stick and brought it back. "Here," was all he said. "We et our fill and I ain't one fer wastin'." Then he climbed into one of their wagons and we heard rummagin' and slidin' sounds.

I didn't pay him much mind. Near up-like the stew smelled even better than it had far away. My mouth set to waterin' and I looked at Pa. He nodded his head and I helped myself to a bowlful. The boys followed close on me, and I set to eatin' what turned out to be even better than what it smelled to be. Things just kept gettin' better. Why even the July heat didn't seem like any kind of trial at all compared to all the good that was happenin'.

Suddenly the rummagin' sounds ended and Mr. Ross climbed out of the wagon with a sack of flour slung over his shoulder and a sack of oats in his hand. "The wife always was one fer carryin' more than we was needin'. Cain't use this. Was goin' to get shed of it so as to make better time a fur piece back." Even though his acts were weepin' with kindness, his words were as brusque-like as ever. He dropped the flour next to Pa and hurried off.

We all stared after Mr. Ross. I think Pa must have been a mite stunned 'cause Mr. Ross had disappeared again into his wagon before Pa stammered a thank you. "It's another miracle," Lije whispered.

"The outside of a man don't always tell you what's inside," Pa said.

Sary and I had worked hard all day helpin' Aunt Hat. We'd scrubbed clothes against the washboard until my knuckles were so red and so raw that now as I washed dishes the soap stung my hands. But I made my mind think on how it would be hangin' out the clothes so I wouldn't think on the hurt in my hands. The washin' and the hangin' took most of the day, but there was still water to fetch and cookin' to help with, but mind you, I'm not complainin'. Why for the first time it somehow didn't even seem like work what with havin' Sary alongside me talkin' and laughin' the whole time. Why it was more like a party than work! I smiled as the picture of Sary hangin' Pa's trousers filled up my mind. She was on the wrong side of the wind and the legs of the trousers kept wrappin' 'round her head so she couldn't see. I laughed till the water rolled out of my eyes, then finally said to her, "If you turn around so your back's to the wind it'll be a mite easier."

"Ya'll could have said somethin' sooner," Sary said.

"I thought you should know better. Haven't you ever hung out washin'?"

"George's ma always done it," Sary said, "and while we've been travelin', we ain't washed much."

That gave me a parcel to think on. My mind had come back to it on and off all day, and now rememberin' it I glanced over to where George was sittin' against the wheel of one of the Ross's wagons. He was alone and starin' out to the east as if he was starin' clean through the mountains and over the plains and was seein' into North Carolina to where his ma and pa were.

Suddenly the sound of Lije and Jed arguin' over the last spoonful of stew brought me back. It wasn't often there was a last spoonful of anythin' to be had and they seemed to be enjoyin' the arguin' as much as the food. Pa finally told 'em that if they were goin' to argue so, *he'd* eat the last stew. That decided 'em on splittin' the remainder in half and things fell quiet again.

I finished washin' the last bowl soon as Lije emptied it and noticed how, with a full belly, I felt that my eyelids were made of lead. Thank goodness Jacob was tired, too. Pa lifted him up into the wagon and he cuddled onto the quilt and was snorin' before I could climb in beside him. But as heavy as my eyelids were, I couldn't sleep. For months I'd been beddin' down in that windowless cabin. That might be nice in the winter when the snows are fallin', but in the spring and summer and all the other times it was torture of the worst kind. Now I was free! I watched the fires flickerin' in the village and listened to the far away voices of the Indians. It was funny how you could hear 'em so good at night and never in the day. Flies and insects sang around me, and the warmth of the stars comin' out in the sky tickled my bones.

I lay back and tried soakin' the moment to the inside of me. My mind set to thinkin' on how there was no way even Aunt Hat could make the inside of a cabin near as beautiful as God made his earth, when I heard footsteps behind the covered side of the wagon. "Millennium?" It was Sary.

"Yes," I whispered back.

"Pa went in to set with Ma fer a spell. Cain I come up with ya'll?"

"Certain sure!"

I gave her a hand and pulled her in. We sat without speakin' for a long time. Lije and Suzanna passed by talkin' low to each other. Sary giggled and so did I. Lije turned and gave me a look that even in the dark I could tell had arrows on it. That made me giggle harder, but I wasn't wantin' to be upsettin' Lije, so I covered my mouth with my hand to muffle the sound and lay down low in the wagon. Now Sary was gigglin' more!

"Ssshhh!" I said. "Lije'll have my hide!"

Sary covered her mouth, but it didn't help none. Finally I figured they were past hearin' and sat up again lettin' the giggles die out normal-like, but then just when I thought I'd gotten rid of the giggles, Sary said, "I think yer brother's sweet on Suzanna. Think I ought to tell him that she snores?" And she started me to gigglin' again. Together we giggled until my ribs hurt and then with a sigh we finally sat still for awhile, except for an occasional chuckle.

For a long time then we sat listenin' to the night sounds and thinkin' our own thoughts. I'd heard once that friends think alike so I took to wonderin' if Sary was thinkin' on how beautiful a place the world is same as me.

But she wasn't. "Millennium's a strange name," she finally broke the silence. "Pa says it means a thousand. Why'd yer folks name ya a *thousand*?"

I sat a moment wonderin' if I wanted to tell and then decided that was just the kind of thing a friend did. "My ma named me Millennium before she died. It's all I've got of my ma, just the name she gave me."

"But why'd she land on Millennium? Why not Jane or Harriet or somethin' ordinary?"

"It's about the only thing Pa's told me. Ma named me Millennium 'cause of some fancy words from the prophet Isaiah in the Bible."

"What words?"

"About a thousand years that's comin'. Isaiah says that in that Millennium the wolf will lie down to rest with the lamb and the kid without even thinkin' on harmin' 'em, and the bear's cub and the cow's calf will play together right friendly-like. Why from what I hear tell, I'll be able to walk right up to a lion and offer him food and he'll eat it out of my hand without eatin' the hand too. And that's another thing! There'll be plenty of food, good food. Why I don't think they'll even have sego lily anyplace—not in the Millennium! And there'll be so much that the rabbits and other critters can eat all day and they won't be eatin' it away from a body."

"I heard ma tell about that!" Sary said. "She read it to us out of her big black Bible."

"There won't be any hate like there is now, neither. Won't be fightin' or hurtin'. No sickness and nobody will be lonely. That's why Ma named me Millennium. She said she was ready for the Millennium, and if the world wouldn't give it to her, she'd at least remind them about it. I'm the reminder. She wouldn't even let the boys shorten it to Milly. Always made 'em call me by my whole name so she could hear it and be reminded of it at least a hundred times a day."

Sary didn't say anythin' for a long time and neither did I. It was a fine night for just lookin' into, especially with a friend by your side. Those long winter nights that I'd filled up with thinkin' about havin' a friend, I'd imagined gigglin' and talkin', but I'd never thought on how havin' a friend meant that even the untalkin' times were company. It felt fine, real fine, just lookin' into the night together.

When she finally spoke, Sary whispered kind a sad-like, "Ya'll got a fine name, Millennium." And then we just sat again watchin' the fires in the village flickerin' out.

I was feelin' more content than our cow, Bluebird, after I've milked her. It had been a long spell since I'd had a friend to be sharin' secrets with. Then suddenly I noticed that Sary was cryin'.

"What's the matter?" I asked.

"Cain't say."

"Don't be tellin' me that again!" I said.

"I cain't say, Millennium."

This wasn't how it was supposed to go—havin' a friend, I mean. Friends were supposed to giggle and tell secrets and play and make dolls out of thistles and corn cobs. Friends made wishes on the stars and promised that they'd be friends forever. But they didn't cry while lookin' at the stars and not tell the reason.

"What do you mean you cain't say? I've just been tellin' you my deepest secret and you tell me you cain't say yours."

"I cain't say," Sary was cryin' hard now.

"Is it your ma?" I asked. "'Cause if it is, Aunt Hat'll take care of her. I told you that."

Sary shook her head, but even before she took to shakin' it, I knew that wasn't the problem. Somethin' more was troublin' Sary. But what?

Suddenly the cabin door opened and Mr. Ross stepped out. Sary jumped. "I'd best git." She wiped at her eyes, sniffed and wiped again.

Quiet as a sliver, she jumped down and started for her wagon. She was almost there before Mr. Ross saw her. "Where ya been, Sary girl?"

"How's Ma?" she asked without answerin'.

"She's still lookin' mighty peaked. But she's comin'. Has to. I's got to set up my store before them miners are all gone and there's no more gold."

"They'll still be there, Pa," Sary said.

"Better be," he said. "Better be." Then he climbed under one wagon and Sary the other.

I lay down tryin' to figure what it was that was troublin' Sary, but the next thing I knew the mornin' was bathin' me in light and another day had commenced.

CHAPTER 7

$\mathcal{I}$T MIGHT HAVE BEEN THE LIGHT THAT FIRST STIRRED ME, but it was definitely the smell that pulled me out of the wagon. Bread, real bread, was bakin'. Lije was hummin'. Jed was dancin'. Pa was grinnin' so big that I knew my nose wasn't playin' any tricks. That smell, sure enough, was bread.

"Mornin', Millennium!" Jed sang out.

I couldn't answer. My mouth had commenced waterin'. I grabbed the bucket and ran for the spring without even thinkin' to change out of my nightdress. "Millennium Boxall!" Pa called, but I didn't stop. Aunt Hat wouldn't be lettin' me get my hands on any of that bread till they were clean so I was needin' water.

I managed to keep most of the water in the bucket despite the trot back and commenced to scrubbin' myself. Even that first cold splash that sent me to shiverin' didn't slow me this mornin'. I was just wipin' my wet face on my nightdress, when Mr. Ross stepped out of the cabin and cleared his throat real loud-like. Us Boxalls were all gathered 'round waitin' for what we was smellin'.

"Mr. Boxall," Mr. Ross said loud and gruff like he always talked. "I's obliged fer what ya'll been doin'. But I's makin' it knowed that this nearness yer wife's brought about ain't changed nuthin'. We might be closer, but seein' as how we're not of the same kind, I'll be grateful if ya'll remember that. I still ain't fixin' to let my family be mixin' with ya'll." He stared at Lije while he spoke and then let his eyes settle on me. I wanted hard to be starin' back, but my eyes fell to the ground.

Pa's leg was jerkin'. But that wasn't the worst. I felt like all that water that had been shiverin' over my skin was now suddenly shiverin' inside me. Sittin' in the wagon next to Sary last night talkin'—and not talkin'— had been the best moment of my life and I'd been thinkin' that's how things would be goin' now they were right here beside us.

"Ya needn't be feared of us," Pa said. "I'd hoped you'd know that by now."

Mr. Ross stared for a moment, switched which foot he was standin' on and bit down on his lower lip. "I do knows that," Mr. Ross said.

"Then what's yer point?" Pa asked.

Mr. Ross looked at Pa hard, but Pa didn't back

down none. He squinted right back. "Cain't say. But I got my reasons."

Hearin' those words again, I swung 'round to find Sary. She was just a few paces behind me. Why could these Ross people never answer?

"The important thing now is takin' care of yer wife. The other things will work out and you can be on yer way. Less said the better," Pa said and I almost shouted, Amen! but I didn't. Pa would have been right proud of how I held my tongue, if he'd known how I was holdin' it.

Just then Aunt Hat opened the door, holdin' three of the most beautiful loaves of bread I'd ever laid eyes on. "We're havin' oats for breakfast," she said in what almost sounded like a song. Mr. Ross was still standin' beside me, and without thinkin' I turned, threw my arms around him and shouted, "Thank-you! Oh, thank-you, Mr. Ross!"

Soon as I finished speakin', I realized my mistake. He looked startled, but he didn't do nothin' but blush and mutter somethin' about it bein' nothin' and walk away fast-like.

"We're all beholdin'," Aunt Hat called after him. Mr. Ross just kept walkin'.

The steam was risin' and the smell was fillin' me so as I could feel myself bitin' into the bread even though it was still on Aunt Hat's platter! Brigham and Aaron 'most knocked Aunt Hat over.

"Settle, boys," Pa called and everyone forgot about Mr. Ross. "We've not blessed this food."

Even I could sense the point of that. After all this was the first meal we'd had in months that was worth sayin' a blessin' over. But I sure hoped Pa called on one of us to do the blessin' so the bread would still be hot when we commenced eatin' it. I was more than a mite relieved when he called on Jed. Jed said the shortest prayers of anyone in the family.

After the prayin' I took a piece and tried to decide how best to be eatin' it. My first thought was to be doin' it fast and hopin' I could talk Aunt Hat into more. But then I figured there wouldn't be more. I might as well be enjoyin' every chew even if it meant the last bites weren't warm. I settled my teeth on the crust, savorin' the crunchin' sound as much as the heat steamin' against my face and the smell fillin' my lungs. Then my tongue picked up on the tastin' part and that's all I noticed. I commenced to chewin', really chewin', not the careful kind of chew that I'd come to know from eatin' the Indians' cornmeal, but a lip smackin', savorin' kind of chew. My stomach growled as if to ask why I was keepin' it waitin', and I swallowed down that first bite so my stomach could be every bit as pleased as my mouth.

Then I noticed that Sary was laughin'. Oh, it wasn't a loud kind of laughin'. But her eyes were twinklin' and her mouth was strainin' to keep from turnin' up at the corners. She was sure enough laughin'. And at me! For a moment all the pleasurin' drained out of me. But it was only a wink before I had my good wits about me again. Like Pa always says, no one can take away your happiness, only you can give it away. Let Sary laugh right out loud if she wanted. I was going to enjoy every bite of that bread. And I did.

By the time I finished, Sary was finished too. Suzanna was helpin' Aunt Hat, and the boys were headin' for the fields with George. Maybe Mr. Ross's speech wasn't goin' to mean much after all. I was feelin' like sunshine itself, but Pa was the surprisin' one. Pa was radiant. Seems like a strange word to be describin' Pa, but at that moment it was the only word that fit. I don't know if it was the bread and the oatmeal mush with real sugar on it or the fact he had two more bodies to help him in the fields. I'd overheard him tellin' Aunt Hat that he was goin' to be able to plant five more acres than what he'd first planned. I saw the look on Aunt Hat's face when he said it and knew that must be awfully good news.

"Millennium Boxall!" It was Aunt Hat's voice.

"Yes, ma'am?" I answered, wonderin' what I'd done now.

"Look at you! Mind, you're still in your night-clothes and walkin' around without an ounce of shame!"

"It was the smell of the bread that plumb sent me into the crazies!" I said and hurried into the cabin to put on my dress. I'd changed the night before in the wagon, so this was the first time I'd seen Mrs. Ross up close. She still looked pale, so pale she almost shined in the darkness. "Mornin', Mrs. Ross," I said.

Her long, brown hair had been braided and the braid was hangin' over one shoulder. She was propped up while Suzanna fed her some of the mush. "Mornin'," she answered weakly.

I couldn't think of anything else to say, but the sound of the spoon against the bowl and her sippin' weak-like at the mush set the willies through me so that all of a sudden I found myself sayin', "Hope yer feelin' better."

She was chewin' slow-like, as if she was eatin' raw potatoes or something that took effort instead of mush, and didn't answer. I'd seen lots of people dyin' before. When we crossed Iowa and wintered in Winter Quarters, death was a common enough visitor. Why I'd seen death come from the blackleg, from the ague, from freezing, from accidents, and from just plain hunger. I'd seen it before and the sick ones were always pale and weak like Mrs. Ross. Suddenly a fear swept into me that maybe even Aunt Hat couldn't help Mrs. Ross.

"You're goin' to get better! Aunt Hat'll see to that!" I said. "You're goin' to be just fine. Why you're goin' to get all pink in the face again and everything's going to be just fine. You'll see. Just fine. Won't be long and you'll be all better."

I pulled my dress over my head while I was speakin' and poked my head out of the neck in time to see Suzanna starin' at me startled-like, but Mrs. Ross went on slowly chewin' as if she hadn't heard.

Just then Aunt Hat came in. "Millennium, I need you to go over to the village and find Katato. I need an herb I think she has. Here's the last sprig of what I had. Take it to her and ask for more." Then Aunt Hat glanced about the room. I knew she was lookin' for somethin' she could trade for the herbs, but we didn't have much. Finally she settled her eyes on a large wooden spoon Pa had carved. "Jed'll make me another," she muttered and handed it to me.

I was speechless. A few times Tew-yu and her ma, Katato, had come here. A few other times, before Tew-yu got married, I'd met up with her in the sunflower fields on the other side of the creek. But as close as we were to the village, I'd never been allowed near it. I'd only watched from here. Now Aunt Hat wanted me to walk right into the village and find Katato and ask her for herbs. Why she didn't speak any more English than Tew-yu did!

It was a strange mix of fear and excitement that took me into its grasp. I'd always wondered what the village looked like up close. But alone? Then I remembered. "Is it all right if Sary comes along?"

"You'll have to ask her ma."

I turned to Mrs. Ross, who nodded.

I grabbed the spoon and ran out the door. Sary was just totin' the milk in from milkin'. "Darned cow!" she muttered. "Stepped on my foot and pert near tipped the bucket over!"

"Want to go to the Indian village with me?" I asked.

"For certain?" Sary asked.

"Certain sure!"

Her excitement made me forget the fear part of what I was feelin', that is until we were within smellin' distance of the village. Then all the fearin' came back and more, but I took a deep breath and swallowed the fear down as best I could, so Sary wouldn't know. There were near twenty teepees in a semicircle facin' to the east, toward the mountains. All the teepees opened that way too. As we drew near we came on mothers cookin', scrapin' hides, hoeing, and nursin' children. To the north there were more mothers workin' in the corn-field. There were more dogs than people, which took to barkin' when they saw us. They were scrawny dogs, but that didn't hinder them from actin' fierce as if they was lions 'stead of just little dogs. Braves were sittin' around as if they were contemplatin' the problems of the world, and in the center of the village a large group of 'em were sittin' in a circle laughin' and playin' some kind of game with a bone. But as soon as any of 'em laid eyes on us, they stopped what they were doin' and stared. Soon even the dogs stopped their ruckus.

Silence began to swallow us up, and I was thinkin' on how Jonah in the belly of that whale couldn't have had it any quieter.

I don't even reckon I know when Sary took hold of my hand, but of a sudden I realized that she was holdin' it tight-like. "I thought ya'll said they was friendly Indians," Sary whispered.

I knew I had to be brave. "They are."

"Don't look it to me."

"They are." I knew I was repeatin', but I couldn't think of anything else. Suddenly I spotted Tew-yu ahead and hurried. Tew-yu's eyes widened as she saw me and she, too, stopped and stared. I took a deep breath, "There's Tew-yu," I said to Sary.

Sary looked in the direction I pointed. She was standin' next to three long poles leanin' together at the top so as to hold a rawhide bag. There was a fire nearby and she was heatin' up rocks about the size of small taters and puttin' them inside the bag.

"What's she doin'?" Sary asked.

I felt a tinge of pride that I knew how to be answerin'. Lije had been here lots of times and he'd told me. "There's soup or stew or somethin' cookin' in that bag. She puts the rocks in to heat it up. She just keeps on heatin' and addin' rocks until the food's hot enough. It's how they cook liquid things."

"That's a silly way to be cookin'!" Sary said. "Why don't they jist get a kettle?"

"'Cause a kettle's awful heavy to be totin' when they move on!"

By then we were standin' next to Tew-yu. "Hello," I greeted. She smiled and some of the fear I'd been feelin' melted away.

"She don't know what 'hello' is," Sary whispered.

"Shhhhh!" I said. Then turnin' back to Tew-yu I held out the herb Aunt Hat had given me. "More?" I asked.

Tew-yu's big black eyes drew into a puzzled expression. She looked at me, then she looked up and down Sary. Sary straightened and looked for a moment as if she would turn tail and run. She didn't, but Tew-yu did. All of a sudden she turned and bolted.

"What did ya do?" I asked Sary.

"I didn't do nothin'! I dared hardly even look to her."

Tew-yu had disappeared inside the tepee. The rawhide cover had been drawn up and tumbleweed and brush had been placed around the poles so air could blow through. I glanced around wonderin' what I should do next, when Tew-yu came out followed by her ma and a young brave.

Tew-yu pointed to me and the brave stepped forward. My heart took to poundin' inside my chest like it was tryin' to get out.

"What want?" the brave asked.

"I want some more of this herb. Aunt Hat needs it

for Sary's ma. She's ailin'."

The brave turned to Tew-yu's ma and said something. Katato sucked her lips into her toothless gums makin' a hole in her face. She must have eaten a lot of that cornmeal, I thought as she said something back to the brave. Then she started across the village and the brave turned back to us. "She get," he said.

Tew-yu stepped forward and pointed to the brave. "Degonda," she said. I'd heard Lije talk of Degonda, Tew-yu's husband. Lije once told me his name meant One Who Speaks. He'd also told me that Tew-yu means One Who Pulls and Katato means Stays at Home.

"Oh," I said. "Degonda." Then I turned to Sary. "This is her husband," I whispered. Sary's eyes went big.

Tew-yu nodded. She never smiled but constantly nodded. I looked at her close and wondered why they called her One Who Pulls, but I couldn't figure it.

Never before had Tew-yu and I had a chance to talk so as to understand each other. "Ask her why she hasn't been out to the sunflower fields?"

Degonda spoke without askin' Tew-yu. "She wife now. Must work."

"Well, tell her I liked it when she came."

Degonda spoke in his own tongue and Tew-yu nodded. Just then Katato came back. She handed me the herbs and I gave her the spoon. She looked at it closely, clicked her tongue, and nodded approval. She spoke to Degonda and he said, "She say to tell mother, when time for baby come, she help."

How did she know? I wondered, but then I realized the herb must be a special one for birthin'.

Most of the Indians had stopped starin' and were goin' back about their business. The fear was still inside me, but the curiosity was growin' so as to be greater than the fear. That made me feel a little braver. Every place I looked a new question came into my head. I hesitated, wonderin' for some excuse to be stickin' around. But Degonda walked away and there wasn't much to do. I waved to Tew-yu and nodded to her ma, hopin' that she'd know that was a thank you and turned to go. Sary still had hold of my hand and instead of lettin' go and turnin', she backed up in a circle till she was on the other side of me and we started off.

I was so busy noticin' Sary's strange behavior I didn't see Tew-yu followin' us. Suddenly she tapped me on the shoulder. I turned and her noddin' head greeted me. When I stopped, she pointed to herself and said, "Learn talk." Then pointin' to where Degonda had gone she added, "Teach."

"Good!" I cried and hugged her to me. She looked startled. Of course the hug was complicated by the fact that Sary was still holdin' to my hand. But when she saw my smile, she nodded again. "Friends!" I said.

"Fre-ends?" she repeated very slowly.

I pointed to Sary and then lifted our clasped hands. Then I took her hand with my other. "Friends," I repeated. Then once more I pointed to her and to Sary and back to me. "Friends. We are friends."

"Ahhh," she said. "Friends."

Degonda then called, usin' those strange words I couldn't understand and Tew-yu turned and ran back to the teepee. For a moment I fell to feelin' a mite sorry for myself seein' that it seemed no one's ma or pa or husband would ever be lettin' them speak with me, when I felt Sary's hand sweatin' in mine. That changed my thinkin' a bit. I decided that I best just worry about each moment. Right now there was a hand in mine. Instead of worryin', I'd best enjoy the moment.

But maybe I should have let go.

CHAPTER 8

"I CAIN'T BELIEVE I'S SET FOOT IN A REAL INDIAN VILLAGE!" We were only half way to the cabin and it was at least the hundredth time Sary'd said that same thing. My ears were tirin' of it!

"Did ya'll see them feathers in their hair?" Sary was usually not much for talkin', but since we'd left the village words had come pourin' out of her like a river. "And to think she's married. I once knowed a girl back home jist a year older than me that's married now. But Ma's says fourteen's a mite too young for marryin'. But Lije was right. Degonda *is* handsome. Oh, wasn't he handsome, Millennium."

"Certain sure!" I replied.

"Oh, I cain't believe I's set foot in a real Indian village! Why I could see right into the inside of that teepee what with the hides pulled up and the bushes 'round it. Did ya'll see that papoose hangin' in its cradleboard from that there pole?"

"Bet ya don't know what the Indians use for dia-perin' their babies." I said.

"What?"

"Dried moss. Lije told me. They just pack it in between the baby's legs there in the cradle board and when it's wet or messed up they take it out and get more. They don't even have to wash the rags."

Sary's eyes went big, "You don't say!"

"I do. Lije said there is lots we can learn from the Indians, but Aunt Hat pointed out that white babies aren't confined to a board so as to keep the moss in place. Jed told her maybe they should be."

Sary looked horrified. "He was just a-joshin,'" I said and started laughin'.

Sary laughed along and then started in again. "Can ya'll imagine such a thing? I's seen them cradle boards on the backs of the mothers, from a distance that is, but I ain't never seed one hangin' from a pole in a teepee. I cain't believe I's been in a real Indian village. Why if my friends back home in Missouri could see this . . ."

"Missouri?" I interrupted. "I thought you hailed from North Carolina?"

Sary stopped. Stopped walkin'. Stopped talkin'. Stopped twistin' on her hair. Her face went pale, and she looked at me as if lightnin' had just struck the both of us.

"I am. Certain sure. I's from North Carolina. That's right. Why I don't reckon why I said Missouri." She started walkin' again, but her *voice* wasn't certain sure no matter what her *words* were sayin'.

I followed behind her. "Sary Ross, I knew you were hidin' somethin' from me! Is this what you couldn't be sayin'? Where were you born?"

"North Carolina."

"The truth?"

"The certain truth."

My mind was spinnin'. I caught up to her, then stepped in front of her so I could see into her eyes. She kept walkin' so I had to be walkin' backwards. "How long did you stay in North Carolina?"

Sary looked at her feet and looked up at the mountains and then at the wagons beside our cabin. She chewed on her lower lip and finally looked back to me. "A month."

"Then you moved to Missouri?"

Sary nodded. "But it don't mean nothin', Millennium. Ya'll are friends now, Millennium. Please don't tell. Honest, it don't mean nothin'."

I stared for a long moment not knowin' what to do.

"Pa'll skin me alive!" she whispered. "Pa said this'd happen. Warned me that with all the talkin' I do . . ." Sary looked at me again, a searchin' kind of look, then she took off runnin' for the cabin.

"Hold up," I called, but she didn't. I ran to catch her.

"Where in Missouri?" I asked, catchin' hold of her

arm and spinnin' her around to face me.

Sary didn't answer. Tears were fillin' up her green eyes and she was chewin' again on her lower lip, lookin' straight ahead as if she didn't hear my words at all.

"Where in Missouri?" I asked again.

"I was born in North Carolina," she said, the tears now runnin' down her cheeks.

I don't know what came over me then. "Here, take these to your ma," I said sharply as I shoved the herbs at Sary, almost knockin' her over. Then I just started runnin'. I ran past the spring and through the creek. I ran into the sunflowers lettin' the acres of yellow swallow me up. I ran till my feet wouldn't carry me another step and my lungs burned. Then I dropped into that yellow. Rollin' onto my back, I stared into the sky and let the strong smell of crushed sunflowers fill my lungs until I felt as if I was chokin'.

Aunt Hat would want me for churnin' and washin' and totin' and tendin', but I had me some thinkin' to do. Finally I knew what it was the Ross family couldn't be sayin', and I wished I didn't know. How could I have a friend from Missouri?

All the memories I had of Missouri came floodin' through my mind mixed with stories that weren't my memories but had become such from all the tellin' I'd heard while we lived in Nauvoo. I saw the men with black faces and the fire, and I heard the shots whizzin'

over our heads and I felt Pa holdin' me, runnin', runnin', runnin' my head bouncin' against his shoulder, and the cold and the trail of red in the white snow when we finally stopped runnin' and he made me walk. It all came back as if I was three again and it was happenin' all over.

And while I was livin' it all over again it suddenly occurred to me that Sary's pa could have even been one of the mobbers that drove my ma away! He could have been one of those men with gunpowder on their faces! Maybe the one whose face kept me awake for years afterwards. Why had I ever wanted a friend? This was worse than bein' lonely had ever been! I had a friend from Missouri!

I tried not thinkin' on it. I picked one of the sunflowers and pulled the petals out of the brown center one at a time. The petals floated down into my face and I blew them away. The white liquid that was oozin' from the broken stem stuck to my hands like honey, but I didn't care. Bees buzzed. Flies swarmed. Sun burned down on me. I shifted my bonnet to keep it out of my eyes and wondered what I was to do next.

Pa was always talkin' on forgivin'. But this was a mighty big thing to be forgivin'. The confusion in my mind swelled up till it was hurtin' my head. Aunt Hat had been wrong. Mr. Ross was mean—not only mean, but a mobber! That's what they were hidin'. That's what they couldn't be sayin'! They were Missourians.

They were mobbers! But then I remembered the bread and Mr. Ross givin' us the fixins. A mobber wouldn't give us sugar and flour, would he? Maybe I was wrong. Maybe he wasn't a mobber, but then I saw Sary's face while she was sayin' she was born in North Carolina, and I knew I wasn't wrong. Why else would they be hidin' where they'd come from?

It hurt so much thinkin' on it that I tried thinkin' on somethin' else. I thought of the trunk and those dishes and that house with wings. I wished hard as I ever had that I lived in that house right now so as I could just fly away in it like a bird. Maybe a house with wings could even take me right into Isaiah's Millennium. But I couldn't keep my mind on it. Always before it worked, but now when I tried seein' that blue house, instead I saw Sary's face, or I'd hear her gigglin' in my ears, or I'd remember the taste of that bread and where it had come from. It was all too confusin'.

I looked around me hopin' for somethin' to fill up my thoughts with and for the first time noticed how thirsty the sunflowers looked. They'd stood so proud like after the spring rains, but there hadn't been any rain since. Now they were wilted and drooped over, even loosin' some of the yellow that made them so pretty. It was exactly how I felt, and instead of distractin' my thoughts, I found myself wonderin' if the sunflowers were somehow respondin' to me rather than to lack of water. Maybe this terrible feelin' was as contagious as the giggles had been for Sary and me. Maybe everythin' was always goin' to wilt and droop and change to somethin' bad when I was around. Like crickets eatin' our food just when we were so needin' it and people drivin' us out of our homes just when we'd built a brick one that was goin' to last forever. Or like finally havin' a friend and findin' out her pa was a mobber. Then I saw those black faces again with anger burnin' bright as the torches in their eyes. My insides ached and my head pounded with all the water pushin' behind my eyes to get out. But it didn't come. It never came. It just pushed and swelled and hurt.

"Millennium?" The voice belonged to Lije and it wasn't far off. However, the sunflowers were tall enough that Lije would never see me unless he stepped right on me. I tried to decide whether to keep hidin' or answer.

"Millennium? I know you're out here. Answer me. Millennium Boxall, where are ya? You've interrupted my chores already, now don't waste more of my time!"

Lije seldom got worked up, but he was gettin' there now. That decided me.

"I'm here." I sat up so as he could see my head.

"What in tarnation are ya doin'?" he asked. "Mr. Ross gave Hat the milk from their two cows plus we've got ours. You got butter to churn, and Jacob needs tendin' to. I should be waterin' not wastin' time..." Suddenly he stopped dead sentence. I don't know if my face was tellin' more than I was wantin' it to, but somethin' stopped him.

"What's the matter?"

I shifted off the rock that was makin' my backside hurt. "Can't say," I found myself sayin'.

"Well, come on. Back to work. Unless you want another winter a starvin', you best be doin' some good. There's no time for sun baskin' and flower gatherin' or don't you remember what it was like last winter?"

"I remember, Lije!" I was gettin' mad at Lije now, and he was my favorite brother, the one I never was mad at.

"Then if you're knowin' it, be doin' somethin' about it. You pert near scared Pa runnin' off like that. Somethin' happen in the village?"

"No."

"Then what's eatin' at ya so?"

"Can't say."

"Tarnation, Millennium!" Lije shook his head. "Glad I've only got one sister to try figurin'." He sat down next to me then but didn't say another word, as if he was waitin'. It was the waitin' that got to me.

"Can people be good and bad all at the same time?" I finally asked.

"That's what people are—good and bad mixed together."

"Why? How? How can they be good *and* bad?"

"Not just people. Everything. The rain's good

when it waters our crops, but it's bad when it floods us. The sun's good when it warms us and bad when it bakes us."

"Like fire. It's good when we use it for cookin' and heatin', but not so good the way the mobbers used it for burnin' our house," I said.

"Exactly. And with people, sometimes it's not even 'cause of a person's tryin' to be good or bad. Sometimes it's a matter of circumstance."

"What do ya mean by circumstance?"

"It's the conditions. Like us here in the desert. We have to take water to the crops in ditches. We do that 'cause the circumstance is we don't have much rain."

"That's what Aunt Hat was talkin' 'bout when she said we hadn't had time for talkin' these past years!"

"Yep, that's circumstance. I heard her tell Pa how she hadn't realized how lonely you were until Sary came. Said she felt bad she hadn't been more of a ma to you, especially when you was the best daughter a woman could ask for."

"Daughter?"

"She said that, sure."

That news almost caused me to forget all that was troublin' me, but not quite.

"Think circumstance could have made some of the Missourians into mobbers?"

"Know it did. Some of them was feared we'd vote against slavery. If we did that they'd lose their slaves, which also meant they might be losin' their farms and for certain their way of livin'. Some of them were feared 'cause our towns grew so fast and others 'cause our ideas of religion were so different than theirs. Some preachers were feared 'cause they thought we'd take away their congregations and then how'd they get paid? Still others were jealous, and some just plain believed the lies that were spread about us. There was a whole bushelful of circumstances."

For a minute I thought Lije was speakin' for the mobbers. But when I looked into his face I knew better.

"I heard Pa speak on it," he went on. "Certain sure some people are smart enough to reason it out and seein' the truth of it are brave enough to stand up to the troublemakers. But not most folk. The hatin' ones stirred up the fearin' ones, and once they were full of that dark hatred, they did all kinds of evil things that they wouldn't normally do. A man's gotta be bigger than the circumstances or they eat him up."

"A woman too?"

Lije laughed. "Certain sure. Ya just got to make the best of whatever circumstance ya find yourself in. It's not always easy."

"Ya know Lije, you're gettin' to talk pert near as fancy as Pa."

Lije laughed and picked a sunflower to twirl between his palms. The white stickiness covered his hands till the flower could stick there without him holdin' to it. "Want to tell me yet why ya ran off like that?"

I didn't want to and felt my body tensin' at the thought. "Sunflower's are wiltin'." I said.

"It's the course of things. Come winter they'll die, but come spring they'll grow back again."

I thought on that, but before I reasoned it out Lije began wipin' his hands on his pants and said, "Well, when you're ready, I'll listen. But now we better get back."

"Reckon so," I said.

Sary was totin' water back from the spring when Lije and I got there. She stopped sudden-like when she saw me and stared as if searchin' deep into my soul. She looked at Lije and then back to me. I knew she was askin' in that stare what I was goin' to do, but I didn't know myself yet. So I looked down at my feet and walked on past her.

I went to the cabin, got the cream, and commenced churnin'. I never before remember work feelin' so good. But besides just the workin', havin' that much cream in the churn felt like the riches of heaven had fallen at our door. I wondered what Pa would say if he knew our good fortune was comin' from a mobber.

I stomped that paddle harder and set my mind on the sound and the smell so as I wouldn't be doin' more thinkin', but it didn't work. My mind just churned same as that cream.

It was then that it hit me what the problem was. Just as Lije said, there was good and bad mixed in *me* just like in everyone else! Part of me said, "Be forgivin' and keep Sary for a friend." But part of me said, "Her pa's a mobber! Mobbers drove us out of Missouri and then from Nauvoo. And no amount of flour or sugar or oats or cream can change that!"

When I thought those thoughts the darkness rose in me so I could feel it heavy in my bones and I wanted to hurt him same as they'd hurt Ma. I wanted Mr. Ross to feel how it was runnin' in the cold and leavin' behind your doll and watchin' your house burn and havin' your ma die. I wanted him to be sufferin' like we'd suffered. It was right that he should!

As the thoughts kept churnin', the darkness settled heavier until suddenly it was as if the only feelin's I'd ever felt in my entire life were bad ones and that they'd all come back heavy and dark and at once to consume me. It scared me, but I didn't know how to shake loose of it. I tried. I tried everythin' I knew to do, but the dark feelin' wouldn't let go of my insides, and all I could think about was hurtin' him like I'd been hurt.

CHAPTER 9

$\mathcal{T}$HE REST OF THAT DAY I CHURNED AND WASHED AND toted until I thought I'd break. But even work didn't chase away the heavy darkness.

"Never seen you work so hard, Millennium," Pa said.

If only he knew!

And then there was Sary. She worked, too, but I don't think she ever laid her eyes away from me. I could tell she was worried, and that look made me all the more confused. I wanted to hurt Mr. Ross, but hurtin' him would be a hurt to Sary, too. I didn't want to hurt her. She wasn't the one who ran us out of Far West!

She'd look at me and I'd think on all we did just the day before, the workin' side by side and the gigglin' and watchin' the stars, and the trip to the village. While thinkin' those thoughts the darkness inside me would begin to leave, and I'd decide to keep the secret—for Sary.

But then I'd see her pa and think about him bein' one of those mobbers, and the darkness would sink right back into my bones and I'd be thinkin' on ways to let him know how it felt. Then my mind would be stuck again, 'cause there was nothin' bad enough to do to him.

Come night I climbed into the wagon bed with Jacob, every muscle in my body achin' and my mind hurtin' worse. There were only two fires in the village tonight, but there was lots of noise, not commotion noise but chantin' sounds. Lije was stopped near the wagon lookin' toward the village.

"What they doin'?" I asked.

"I don't reckon I know. Must be some kind of ritual."

"Ritual?"

"Yep. They dance and chant prayers and sing to the Great Spirit askin' him to help them. It's their way of prayin'. I don't know though. Maybe that's not it at all. Maybe someone died or was born or it could be anything."

I remembered last spring when there'd been a whole night of noise and drums and the next day was when Lije had found out it was a Bear Dance for Tew-yu. The Indians held the Bear Dance whenever a girl turned into a woman. It was a ceremony to let everyone know that she was now ready to be a wife. It was shortly after that when she married Degonda. Aunt Hat had shaken her head and pinched her lips together in that way she has of doin' and said, "She's too young to be married. Too young for bearin' children."

Pa's face was lookin' like he agreed, but he said, "They got different ways, and we need to be understandin', Hat."

"I know that, Mr. Boxall," Aunt Hat said and went on about her work.

"Sure is interestin'," Lije said. "I can't abide by some of the Indian ways, like stealin' and sellin' children to the Spaniards to be slaves and leavin' their old people to die when they move on."

"Pa said they do that 'cause they don't have enough food."

"I know. I know. But it still sits uneasy in me. But there are some Indian ways I'd sure like to know more about."

"Like what, Lije," I asked.

"Like the way they live in peace with the earth. Instead of livin' on the land, like we do, they're part of it."

Lije crawled up in the wagon box and sat 'side me as he used to back in Winter Quarters when we were waitin' to come west. Jacob was driftin' off, and I snuggled next to Lije's shoulder even though it was a mite hot for snugglin'. With all the worryin' I'd been doin' it was comfortin' just to be near Lije. The way he climbed in there I was expectin' him to be sayin' somethin', but he just stared out at the village for the longest time.

Finally I said, "You've been workin' hard. You missin' your book learnin'?"

"I am," Lije said. "I was hopin' to read law. I once saw a lawyer named Abraham Lincoln arguin' a case in Quincy. He was tall and as skinny as Aunt Hat, but he was a mighty fine man with words. I spoke with him afterwards and he told me to just keep readin'. Said he'd learned the law 'most by himself and that I could too. Only thing, I don't know what law there will be to practice out here."

"It's them circumstances gettin' in yer way," I said and Lije chuckled.

"Reckon so, Millennium."

"Lije, can we make our own circumstances?"

"Reckon so. I think that's what Mr. Lincoln was tellin' me. That he made his own."

He was quiet again for a little while. Then he turned to me as if he was rememberin' somethin'. "What circumstance's been eatin' at you today?" he asked.

"Can't say."

"You can tell me. I'm your brother."

"No. I can't tell no one yet." But I knew Lije and he'd just keep askin' and questionin' until he knew what he wanted to be knowin'. I only had one hope of keepin' my secret until I knew which part of me should win out. I'd keep his mind on other matters.

"You been workin' with George in the fields. Does he talk much about them sellin' away his ma and pa?"

"Did today. First time he's spoken on it."

"While we were eatin' supper I saw him laughin' at ya. First time I've seen him smile since he came."

"He's a hard worker," Lije said slowly. "Don't say much, but today he suddenly stopped workin' and took to lookin' the way they'd come and said, 'I wonder what my old pappy's doin' now.'"

"It ain't right," I said.

"No, it's not, Millennium. It's not right at all, but then there's a lot that's not right in the world, anyway from my way of thinkin'."

"When you're a lawyer you can put things to right, Lije."

"Wonder if things'll ever be to right." he said, but not like he was sayin' it to me.

"What can a body do 'bout all the things that're wrong, Lije?"

"Don't reckon I know. I can't change slavery, or mobbin' either. But I thought on it lots while we was coming West. I decided that if every person did what their heart told them was the right thing to do, despite the circumstances, after awhile the wrongs would disappear. Things would soon enough work out for folks."

"You mean so as there would be no more hatin' and no more fearin'?"

"Yep, but it'd take a miracle."

"That's a mighty fancy idea, Lije. Sounds like Isaiah's Millennium."

Lije chuckled again.

I could feel Lije's heart against my cheek and suddenly realized that it was beatin' in time to the Indian drums. Then I noticed that the stars were winkin' that same rhythm as if heaven and earth were all united in one song. It filled me up with a comfortin' kind of warmth.

"The Millennium will be nice won't it, Lije?"

"Most likely I'll never know," Lije said.

"But we can practice for it."

"Yep. And that's a mighty fancy idea you got there yourself!"

Once more we settled into listenin'. This time Lije broke the spell by laughin' right out loud.

"What ya thinkin' on now?" I asked.

"Just thinkin' on the strange look Degonda had on his face today when he came nose to nose with George. I reckon he'd never seen a black man before. He came into the fields while we were workin'. He usually takes to callin' us squaw-boys and laughin' that we're doin' women's work. But when he saw George, he clean forgot about teasin' and went right over and ran his hand through George's hair. Startled George a mite."

The thought sent me to chucklin'.

"Why, George's eyes opened so wide they pert near filled up his face. He didn't dare speak and he didn't dare move. Degonda always has a big knife in his belt and only that piece of rawhide around his middle and the feathers in his hair. He was big and fierce lookin'. It's a good thing he wasn't painted or George might have fainted dead away."

"What happened?"

"George just stood there paralyzed-like. I think at first he was feared that Degonda was goin' to scalp him. But when Degonda had felt all he wanted, he took hold of his own braid and offered it to George."

I could imagine the difference in Degonda's shiny straight hair and George's curly hair. I chuckled again.

"That startled George even more, but only for a second. Then he commenced to laughin' uneasy-like at first and then a mite more relaxed he took one hand and felt at his own hair while the other felt at Degonda's. 'They might both be black, but they's as different as night is from the day,' George kept sayin.'"

There was only one fire in the village now, and the noise was gettin' louder. Mr. Ross kept crawlin' nervous-like from under his wagon to look. Most everyone else was bedded down now. But Lije didn't show signs of movin'. I didn't mind none. Somehow when he was near the darkness inside me wasn't nearly so heavy.

"You still haven't told me what it is you're not tellin' me," Lije suddenly said.

"Can't say."

"You already said that."

"Still can't say."

"You're sure?" Lije asked. "You been stewin' so, I thought maybe you'd have a hankerin' to be talkin' with somebody."

I turned my face away from Lije and said again, "Can't say." And the heavy feelin' which had started to ease away while I was talkin' to Lije filled me up again with its darkness.

"Sure?" he asked.

"Certain sure."

Lije climbed out of the wagon and started away. "Night, Millennium," was all he said.

I watched him disappear into the night and just as I couldn't see him, I almost called him back, even opened my mouth to be doin' it, but the words wouldn't come out. I settled down in the wagon bed, looked up at the stars, and tried to pray. But the words just seemed to stick in my throat. Once again the sound of the drums and the rhythmic chantin' of the voices was growin' so loud it seemed to fill up the whole night. Finally my eyes grew so heavy I couldn't watch stars anymore. I closed my eyes, and hoped that somehow when I wakened next mornin' there would be an answer in my brain instead of just questions. Most of all I hoped that the sun would chase away the darkness inside of me as it did the night.

CHAPTER 10

*T*HE NEXT DAY THINGS WEREN'T BETTER. THE SUN DIDN'T even come out! For the first time in weeks the sky was clouded completely over so as to make everythin' gray and heavy-like. But it wasn't a rainin' kind of cloudy, only a gloomy kind of cloudy. The hot was hotter than it had ever been, makin' everything sticky, especially me. The war inside me waged on and I worked even harder tryin' to make it all go away. But it didn't help none.

The clouds were holdin' aromas close to the earth so that I could smell the sunflowers even from the cabin and I kept fightin' the urge to run off and soak myself in their bright yellow. But I knew Pa or Lije would just come after me, so I kept on workin'.

It was after lunch when Aunt Hat brought Jacob to me. "Millennium, I am grateful for all your help," and she even reached out and patted me on the arm in her awkward kind of way. I'd always wanted her to do that, but now for some reason I pulled away and stepped back. She looked startled and I felt bad, but didn't know what to do. My body seemed to be doin' things my mind hadn't first thought up, feelin' things my mind wouldn't have thought of.

"Something wrong, Millennium?" she asked.

"No." But I said it too loud, too sharp.

Aunt Hat looked at me hard then put her hand to my forehead.

"I ain't sick."

"You aren't sick," she corrected.

"I ain't sick!" And I backed up another step wonderin' why I was talkin' like that just when Aunt Hat was actin' like a ma acts. Wasn't this what I had always wanted? She'd always been so busy with the little ones that she hardly had time to give me the notice I hankered for. Now here she was noticin', so why was I defyin' her so? I wasn't makin' any sense even to myself and I could see in her eyes that I certain sure wasn't makin' any sense to her.

"I'm just hot." I finally said.

"You've been workin' too hard."

"I'm strong. I can work harder."

Aunt Hat looked back to the fields where Pa and the boys were waterin' and George and Mr. Ross were plowin'; then she turned back to me. Her face looked pained—no it was more of a hurt—and I suddenly realized I'd put the look there. What was happenin'? Why was I actin' like this?

"Well, you've worked hard enough for now. I want you to take Jacob and cool him off in the creek. I'll send out Sary and Suzanna too. You could all use a bath. The men are far enough out they won't see if you go where the willows are thickest. I'll tend to Mrs. Ross and call you when you're needed." She handed Jacob into my arms and hurried back to the cabin, callin' to Sary and Suzanna as she went.

My mind kept urgin' my feet to run again, but with Jacob in my arms I couldn't. I felt like a rabbit caught in one of Lije's traps. The darkness inside me was turnin' to hot lava and boilin' so that I wanted to scream out as loud as I could. But just as I almost did, Jacob put his arms around my neck and kissed my cheek. "I wuv Milly!" he said and kissed me again so that somehow I couldn't scream.

Slowly I turned and started for the creek. Jacob wiggled out of my arms and walked along beside, stoppin' to examine every ant and weed and rock we passed. I kept urgin' him on, but by the time we reached the creek I could see Sary and Suzanna hurryin' toward us, pullin' Robert along between 'em. Robert and Suzanna were gigglin' but Sary—well, she wasn't.

I hurried into the willows and Jacob waded into the water. It was pretty shallow, barely even came to my ankles. I began pilin' rocks at one end to dam up the water. Jacob followed and began pullin' little rocks the size of his fist out of the creek and addin' 'em to my pile. Normally I would have laughed as I watched him copyin' what I was doin', but for some reason it made me mad. "I can do it!" I said and Jacob looked up into my eyes as if he was searchin' for somethin'.

Just then Sary and Suzanna stepped through the willows and joined us. Robert ran right in with Jacob. He was a year older than Jacob, but they'd taken to bein' good friends in the time the Rosses had been here. Immediately Robert also began diggin' for rocks and addin' them to the dam.

"My rock is bigger than yours!" Robert called and threw it down with a big splash.

Suzanna laughed as the water hit mostly on her. "Doesn't matter the size," she said. "Come on, we can make a regular pool like the queens in Egypt has!" And soon everyone was pilin' rocks and the water began backin' up till it wasn't long before it came to our knees.

All this time I was stayin' apart, keepin' out of their way and yet still pretendin' to be helpin'. But out of the corner of my eye I was watchin' Sary who was watchin' me.

Suzanna was sixteen and prettier than Sary. She'd spent most of the time since they came inside with Aunt Hat and her ma so this was the first I'd been with her much. Outside here she seemed like a different person, younger, lighter. Then I figured that inside she was always worryin' about her ma. She laughed with Jacob and Robert and splashed. Then when she was so wet it shouldn't have mattered, she took off her dress and hung it over the willows so she could swim in her underclothes. Sary followed. Their underclothes were white with fancy crocheted trim all around the edges. When I first saw their elegant underclothes, fire burned in me. It wasn't fair that mobbers children had such fine things. Maybe I'd have lacy underwear if we hadn't been burned out and if we had time to make things instead of just tryin' to keep alive! It wasn't right!

"We had a real brick house in Nauvoo!" I suddenly said without even knowin' why. "Red brick with an upstairs for all the bedrooms and a downstairs with a parlor and a kitchen. It even had closets and a spring-house just out the back door."

Suzanna didn't even look at me while I was talkin'. "Ya'll will have another one here some day, I's sure," she said as she sat down in the water.

"We only lived in it a year and they drove us out."

Sary stopped and looked at me. "The house you build here, it'll be just as fine, maybe nicer," she said.

Suzanna talkin' was one thing. She didn't know that I knew. But Sary knew. How could she be talkin' about fine houses when she knew that her pa might have burned us out of our house in Missouri?

"Come on down," Suzanna cried. "It's cool and wet! Feels good!" She tugged on Sary's pantaloons.

Just before we left Nauvoo Aunt Hat had set to makin' pantaloons that she said she'd crochet on. They were to be my first fancy underwear. But they never did get crocheted on, and I was still wearin' 'em even though they were a mite too little and full of holes.

"Take yer dress off, Milly!" Suzanna called. "It's nicer bathin' with it off. No one's gonna see. Water's wonderful. Why I might never git out!"

"Her name's Millennium!" Sary said before I could.

But I heard 'em call her Milly."

"Only Jacob!" I said.

"Sorr-rry!" Suzanna said and then began floatin' leaves to Robert and Jacob and ignorin' Sary and I.

I turned and waded upstream a ways. "Don't ya want to take off yer dress?" Sary asked as she followed me.

"No," I answered. "I always bath with it on!" and I sat down in the water.

Sary sat beside me, looked to see what Suzanna was doin' then turned back to me and began whisperin'. "Look, Millennium, we might not get to talk much. I's got to be tellin' ya that I couldn't sleep all night for thinkin' on ya. Why even the Indian drums didn't bother me as much as my own thoughts. I tried thinkin' on how I'd feel if I found out the people whose ma ya were tryin' to save might be the people who caused yer own ma to die. I wished hard I could change it, really I did."

She waited for me to be sayin' somethin', but I couldn't or didn't. I wasn't sure which.

"Millennium, Pa's changin'. He told us jist last night that he'd been wrong about Mormons."

"He can't change what he did," I forgot to whisper and Sary jerked back to see if Suzanna had heard. She didn't seem to have noticed.

"So are ya goin' to tell?" Sary was rubbin' at her leg and twistin' at her hair. "It'll only make fer trouble. Some secrets is better kept."

"I don't know yet. I can't make up my mind what the right thing to be doin' is."

"But we're *friends*," Sary said.

For two years I'd wished to be hearin' those words and now I was hearin' 'em and it wasn't even pleasin'. I splashed water onto my face to cool it down and then lay right back in the water so I could see through the willows up to the dark, gray sky.

"Think it'll rain?" Suzanna had waded over to us.

"No. Nothin' good's comin' from those clouds." I answered her.

"Ya never know. Sometimes a lot of good comes out of what looks to be bad. Lije told me that himself last night while we were walkin'."

"Pa told ya not ta go walkin' with Lije!" Sary said.

I sat up at the mention of Lije and water poured over my face.

"Lije is a fine man," Suzanna said. "Wants to be a lawyer man. If Pa knowed him better, he wouldn't object to us walkin' nights."

I didn't like the way she was talkin' about Lije, and I didn't like the way her eyes were lookin' while she was talkin' about Lije. Especially with her bein' so beautiful and all. Why what if Lije was taken in by her and him not knowin' what she was? There was one more reason to be tellin'.

Then suddenly 'fore I knew what had happened Suzanna began throwing water and Jacob and Robert joined in. I backed off and tried to stay out of it, but Jacob kept runnin' to me carryin' handfuls of water that he'd scoop up, but by the time he got to me and threw there wasn't any water left. But he'd laugh as if it was the best joke and then he'd splash. I tried real hard not to laugh back, but he just kept on throwin' dried up water and soon I began smilin'.

Then Sary started throwin' water at me. I tried stayin' mad, but when I looked at her drippin' there in her fancy underwear and her hair danglin' wet makin' her look like a lost puppy dog, I just started laughin'. Before I knew it I was throwin' water back and we were havin' the best time. The heavy feelin' washed right out of me and instead of thinkin' about Sary bein' from Missouri, I just thought of her bein' there in the creek with me. Soon Jacob and I took up sides against the Rosses, only Sary seemed at times to be helpin' us more than her own kin.

The cool water ran over me and the breeze which was hot and dry when I was out of the water was now coolin' and refreshin' so that it was hard to remember that it was July and that we were in the desert. We played until we dropped into the pond again and let the water cover us all over except for our faces.

"I love water!" Suzanna cried, liftin' a handful and lettin' it drop into the pond. "Think of all the things a body can do with it! Just think. Why I'll bet some poet has written poems about water that would make ya feel the wet and taste it too. Soon as we get to California I'm goin' to find me a library and read every book until I find the best water poems and then I'm going to memorize 'em and every time I say 'em or think 'em or read 'em, I'm going to remember this moment."

"It would be easier to write yer own!" Sary said.

"Nah, I don't have a way with it, like you do," Suzanna said. "But you can write me one. A real pretty one."

"You write poetry?" I asked.

Sary blushed and Suzanna answered, "She does. Purty poetry too. Ma says Sary can put words together so as to make music come out of them."

Suddenly I realized that there was a whole lot

about Sary that I still didn't know and I wanted to know it. Had she ever had a doll she loved 'most like it was human? If she liked writing poetry, certain she liked readin' much as I did. What books had she read? I was almost to ask her, but then I thought about Ma—Lije said she's the one that taught him to love books— and the swellin' began achin' behind my eyes again. But now, for some strange reason, I could hear Lije's voice sayin' over and over, "Circumstances. Circumstances. Circumstances." It kept on like that goin' around and around in my head until it made me dizzy.

"What ya thinkin' on so hard?" Suzanna asked. "Lately Sary's been thinkin' hard too. I say she's thinkin' on your brother Jed."

"I am not!" Sary cried and threw a handful of water on her sister. "You're the only Ross thinkin' on one of Millennium's brothers."

Suzanna laughed and threw water back on the both of us and the water fight began again, but this time Aunt Hat's voice interrupted the fun. "Girls," she called from the cabin. "It's time to come in."

Sary and Suzanna climbed up the bank and began wringin' water from their underclothes. It was harder for me to be climbin' out what with my dress fully soaked so as to pull me down like a weight, but as I stumbled up the bank I noticed that the heavy darkness inside me wasn't near as bad and I sure liked havin' the heaviness outside of me instead of in. Jacob and Robert knocked down the dam and the water settled low again.

Suzanna stepped where there was grass so as not to get her feet all muddy, but Sary didn't seem to care.

"Come on, Robert," Suzanna grabbed her brother's hand and pulled him out of the water and the way she giggled at him I could see that she loved him like I loved Jacob. I picked Jacob up and he shook his head so that water sprayed all over me.

Suzanna laughed. "He's just like Robert!"

"Those are nice underthings you're wearin'," I said as I squeezed water out of Jacob's pants.

"If we're here a spell, I can show ya'll how to crochet edges like this," Suzanna said. "It's easy."

By then Sary and Suzanna had their dresses back on and we headed back to the cabin, feelin' the heat gradually dry us out. I held my skirt up so it wouldn't get muddy and Jacob ran on ahead. Suddenly thunder sounded, a far away rumblin'—but loud. Sary squealed.

"I didn't expect that!" And she took to gigglin'.

Suzanna laughed too and without helpin' it I joined in.

That was the moment, while we were all laughin', that I made my decision. Sary was my friend and I wanted it to stay that way. And at that moment, even

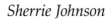

though there was no sun, I could feel the darkness bein' chased right out of my bones. Land a mighty! I knew, certain sure, that I wouldn't ever tell anyone our secret. That was best. After all that's what friends were for.

CHAPTER 11

$\mathcal{T}$HE NEXT MORNIN' I WAS STIRRED OUT OF SLEEPIN' BY THE clangin' of kettles, horses neighin', and whispered shushin'. I opened one eye enough to see the purple over the mountain that meant the sun would soon be up, just comin' out of the black. Not time for gettin' up yet. I shut my eye again and then slowly realized that what I was hearin' wasn't a dream. I listened more and realized it wasn't the sound of the day comin' alive either. This was the sound of life tryin' not to be heard. I listened again to make sure I wasn't dreamin'. But by then there wasn't any sleep left in me. I couldn't be dreamin'.

I peered over the wagon side to see what was goin' on and saw the Ross's wagons packed up. Mr. Ross and George were hitchin' the horses and Sary and Suzanna were loadin' the last few blankets into the wagon.

Suzanna was cryin', not with her voice, but with her eyes.

Suddenly the sleepiness fell out of my brain and like trees fallin' it hit me what was goin' on. "Sary can't go!" I said right out loud and jumped out of that wagon and ran into the cabin. "Pa, Pa," I called. "Come quick!"

"What is it?" Through the darkness I sensed the alertness jolt into him. "What's happened?"

"It's Mr. Ross. He's fixin' to leave."

"What?" it was Aunt Hat's voice.

"Come see. They're packed. Hitchin' the wagons."

"What?" Aunt Hat said again. By now Pa was pullin' on his pants and comin' out the door all at the same time.

"What's goin' on?" he asked.

Mr. Ross froze. He was leanin' over holdin' a horse's hoof between his knees examinin' it. Slowly he set the leg down and slowly he raised to standin'. Even slower he turned to face Pa. Suzanna and George stopped cold, watchin' Mr. Ross. Sary, was watchin' me.

"I was hopin' you wouldn't stir till I came in fer Mrs. Ross."

"What's goin' on?"

"I's a-fixin' ta move on."

"What?" Pa said. "Mrs. Ross can't go now!"

"I aim ta make her comfortable."

Pa shook his head and finished pullin' on his suspenders. "Why?"

"It's time to be movin' on," he said louder.

"That gold can't mean more to you than your own wife!" Pa was near to shoutin' himself.

"It ain't the gold!" Mr. Ross said, his eyes glarin'. "I knows what I's doin'. Now git out of mah way. The woman'll do fine."

"She's in no condition for traveling." Aunt Hat was at the door now clutchin' a shawl around her nightdress. "I can't let you take her. It'll kill her."

"She's my wife and ya'll cain't stop me," Mr. Ross said. "I wouldn't even try if'n I was you." And he looked at his gun hung on his saddle.

I'd been watchin' Pa and Mr. Ross, but suddenly I looked to Sary and was surprised to see tears fallin' down her cheeks. It was then I figured what had happened. Somehow Mr. Ross knew that I knew.

I ran to Pa and stood in front of him facin' Mr. Ross.

"Not now, Millennium," Pa said tryin' to move me over.

"Pa doesn't know. I haven't told him."

"Know what?" Pa asked. "What's goin' on here?"

Mr. Ross pricked like an animal that knows it's bein' stalked. His hand went up to his saddle where his rifle was and he looked hard at me.

I went on talkin' to Mr. Ross. "I know one thing though. It won't make any difference to Pa when he knows. So you don't need to be movin' out."

"You can't go." Aunt Hat said again. "Mrs. Ross won't make it!"

"Millennium, will ya tell me what it is I don't know!" Pa's voice was a strained kind of patient.

I looked hard into Mr. Ross's eyes. At first he stared back and then he looked away, looked to Pa. It was then that a terrifyin' thought struck through me sure as if an ax had cut into me. His eyes were reflectin' everythin' bad I'd felt—the darkness, the heaviness in my insides. The wantin' to hurt someone.

"Get out of my way," he spit out the words.

"I tell ya, it'll be all right," I said louder. "Let me tell him and you'll know what I'm meanin'."

Mr. Ross looked back to me, squinted, looked back toward the cabin, and I knew he was thinkin' about Mrs. Ross. Slowly he turned back to me, but some of the darkness had gone out of his eyes. He stared at me for a long moment, but this time I stared right back.

"It'll be all right," I said again and this time he nodded.

I turned so's I could see Pa and Mr. Ross all at the same time. "Pa," I said slow and careful like, while clingin' for all I was worth to the hope that all I knew about Pa was really true. "They don't hail from North Carolina like they say. They're from Missouri."

Pa looked hard at me. "That the truth?" he asked and I nodded.

"It is," Mr. Ross said, nervous-like, his hand still

restin' on his gun. "And now I'll be movin' on."

I held my breath, still watchin' Pa, half expectin' his leg to be jerkin'. He stared for a long moment and then looked back toward the cabin. Finally he turned back. "There's no need," Pa said softly.

I let the breath out of me, and my heart went to skippin' all inside of me. I was right. Pa's words on for-givin' weren't just words!

But Mr. Ross tightened his grip on his gun and looked toward the place where Lije and the boys were sleepin'. They weren't stirrin'. The Indian village that had beat steady as a heartbeat for two nights was silent. Even the insects weren't soundin'.

"My boys aren't goin' to be hurtin' you and nei-ther am I. You have your reasons for lyin' to us. I don't even want to know them. What I do know is that a woman's life is hangin' on us carin' for her. George, unhitch the horses. Sary and Suzanna get your things back out here. You're not leavin' . . ."

"But you don't understand," Mr. Ross said. "I's not jist from Missouri, I's from Jackson county."

"I said I didn't want to hear it," Pa spoke firm, but not loud.

"Millennium, quick," I hadn't even noticed that Aunt Hat had left the doorway. Now she was comin' back through it, fast-like—and carrying a bucket. A scream came from the inside, not a loud one, but a sick animal kind of screamin'. "Get me some water," Aunt

Hat ordered.

"Mr. Ross, I need lanterns. Mr. Boxall, get the boys, I need a fire. All this commotion!" And Aunt Hat was gone as fast as she came.

I grabbed the bucket and ran. I don't think I ever ran so fast in my life. I was back with the water, what I hadn't spilled for hurryin', and handed it in to Aunt Hat. Everyone, exceptin' Lije and Jed who were startin' a fire, was gathered around the door to the cabin standin' almost in a half circle. It looked so strange-like for so many people to be standin' without movin' that I almost laughed, but I remembered in time what was happenin' and stopped myself.

The screamin' had changed to a moanin'. The lantern was burnin' inside the cabin so as to make a post of light shine where the door was ajar. Mr. Ross had taken off his hat and was wringin' it in his hands. Sary and Suzanna were holdin' each other. Sary's face was white and the tears were tricklin' down her cheeks. George stood back aways holdin' onto Robert, his face filled up with sadness.

Soon Aunt Hat appeared in the post of light again. She was still in her nightdress only there was no shawl now. "Looks as if we're going to have a birthing. I can't do anything more to stop it. It's a mite early, but with the good Lord's help . . ." She looked at Mr. Ross and never finished what she was sayin'. She seemed tired even though it was just comin' on to mornin'.

There was another scream and Aunt Hat disappeared into the light.

"We can't be stewin' here," Pa said. "I'll help ya unhitch those wagons, Mr. Ross. You girls get some breakfast fixed up."

Sary and Suzanna looked at the door that was closin'. But the closin' didn't hold back the sound. Pa must have seen the look in their eyes same as me 'cause he walked over to 'em, put a hand on each of their shoulders and said soft and gentle-like, "Mrs. Boxall is the best midwife in the territory. Your ma is goin' to do just fine. Now the best thing for us is to keep busy. The time'll pass a fine shade quicker that way."

They didn't move. "Hear?" Pa asked.

Slowly Sary looked up at him. "Sure?" she asked.

I ran to Pa's side. "No one can take better care of yer ma than Aunt Hat. Sure as certain," I said.

Suzanna wiped her eyes on the back of her hand and Sary let go of her. They still looked at the windowless cabin as if they were seein' right inside. But they started toward the wagon. I was turnin' myself, when I saw that only Mr. Ross was left standin' still. He clutched at his hat until his knuckles were white. Pa was walkin' toward the fire but stopped when Mr. Ross spoke. "Why ya'll doin' this?"

Pa turned slowly back. "Doin' what?"

"Carin' for my Ginny like she was yer own kin?"

"We're all God's children."

"But ya'll don't understand. I told ya, I's not jist from Missouri, I's from Jackson County, and I was part of the mobs that drove Mormons out of Far West."

Pa stiffened and his leg took to jerkin' as Mr. Ross went on. "I was young and I heard all them tales 'bout the evil ways of the Mormons and got het up. When Gov'ner Boggs issued the order to get shed of every Mormon in the state or ta kill 'em, I felt it my duty ta do all I could."

Pa's leg was still jerkin' and his voice was tight. "I told you once that I didn't want to hear on it. Sometimes it's best to let the past lie in the past."

"But ya don't understand. What if'n I was one of the ones that drove ya out? What if'n it was 'cause of me that yer wife died?" And he started cryin'. I never thought I'd see such a sight as a man that big and ornery-soundin' cryin' soft and gentle like a baby.

"Pa?" I waited. He didn't answer me, but I noticed that his leg had stopped its movin' about.

"That was then," Pa said softly.

Mr. Ross didn't say anything more. He wiped his nose on a big red handkerchief and sobbed back the cryin' until he had it almost stopped. For a long awkward moment he stared at Pa and me. "I don't have no words."

"You don't need any," Pa said and walked away.

Mr. Ross watched Pa leave and then walked to the cabin door and commenced waitin'.

I caught up to Pa. "You don't hate him?" I asked. "What if he was the very one that threw that torch and burned the cabin?"

Pa looked at me now. "He might have been, Millennium. But me hatin' him for it won't bring your ma back. It won't change a thing in the past. It'll only make the future harder to live in."

I looked over at Sary and Suzanna who were pouring oats into a black kettle over the fire. George was takin' the bridle off of the horse. Such an odd mix of folk, I thought. George whose ma was sold. Me, whose ma was dead. Sary whose ma was moanin' on the inside of the cabin. Now here we were together in the middle of a desert. More feelin's jolted through me, but I couldn't put words to any of them.

Suddenly the door opened. Aunt Hat's face was pale. "Suzanna, I know you're a mite young, but I'm needin' you. Millennium run to the village and fetch Katato."

I stared at her. "Quick!" she yelled and turned, leavin' the door open for Suzanna.

CHAPTER 12

$\mathcal{T}$HE NEXT THING I KNEW I WAS RUNNIN'. RUNNIN' HARDER than I ever had run. I reached the village and the teepee that belonged to Tew-yu's family before fear had time to settle over me.

"Degonda? Degonda?" I called.

The brush that had been piled around the bottom of the teepee pushed out and a brown hand appeared. Slowly Degonda's sleep-filled face followed.

"What want?" he asked.

"I need Tew-yu's ma. The baby is comin' and Aunt Hat needs help. Get Katato quick."

"Must talk slow," Degonda said, squintin' his eyes and shakin' his head.

"The baby is comin'," I tried to slow down. "We need Katato."

There were voices inside the teepee and then Tew-yu and her ma crawled out. Degonda followed.

"Come!" I motioned. "Aunt Hat needs help."

I started to run and then stopped, motionin' again for them to follow. They started, but not fast enough to suit me. "Come on!" I shouted again. Faces began peerin' out of the teepees. I couldn't understand the words, but the anger didn't need any language for me to be understandin' it.

The dawn was breakin' full now. "Come quick!" I shouted and then began runnin'. I stopped again and looked back to make sure they were followin'. They were. I turned and ran until I reached the cabin.

Suzanna was just goin' in with a bucket of water. Sary was leanin' against the cabin.

"Aunt Hat! Aunt Hat!" I shouted. "They're comin'. Katato's comin'."

I leaned beside Sary tryin' to catch my breath. Tew-yu, Degonda, and Katato were near now. "Go inside," I said to Katato. Degonda repeated the words so she could understand. Slowly she went to the door and then walked in.

Tew-yu and Degonda sat on the ground. I took in a big breath and it was then that I saw Sary's face. All the days I'd been thinkin' on havin' a friend I'd been thinkin' on what a friend would do for *me*. Never had I thought on how havin' a friend meant doin' for *her*. But now Sary needed me. That thought felt as good as talkin' under the stars in the wagon bed. But it was woven tight with another feelin'—a strong feelin' of helplessness. Sary needed me, but what could I do? I could try speakin' some comfortin' words, but words seemed empty now. It was another one of those circumstances Lije was talkin' on! What word could make the color come back into her face? What word could make her twist at her hair again? But words were all there seemed to be.

"Aunt Hat's better than a doctor," I said. "See this here scar. I cut my finger on Lije's knife once. It bled till I thought there wasn't no more blood in me, and Aunt Hat she sewed it up with that thread of hers."

I didn't tell her how much it hurt when she put her quiltin' needle in to sew it. I figured that with a friend, not sayin' some things was as important as sayin' other things.

Sary didn't move. "Suzanna said the baby's turned wrong. Ma keeps screamin'," Sary said in a whisper that shook like wind rustlin' in a tree.

"Aunt Hat'll know what to do. And especially now that Katato is with her. Katato knows all the Indian medicine. Certain sure she's as good as Aunt Hat. And what with Aunt Hat knowin' white man medicine and Katato knowin' Indian medicine, sure as certain they'll know what to do for yer ma!" But just as I said it there was another scream from the cabin. Sary's face tightened and her body stiffened. Everyone stopped the fidgety things they were doin' and looked at the cabin. I took Sary's hand and held it tight-like.

Suzanna opened the door, started to step out, and then collapsed into a heap. Mr. Ross ran to her and gathered her up in his arms, carryin' her to the wagon.

"She all right?" Aunt Hat called out.

"We'll take care of her," Pa called back.

The sun was up now, startin' its journey across the sky. I kept watchin' it climb farther away from the mountains and wonderin' how much longer we'd have to be waitin'.

When I'd come back from the village everyone was backed off aways from the cabin, but they kept steppin' closer. Lije and Aaron had Brigham and Jacob. George was still holdin' to Robert. Even the little boys were standin' rigid as pine trees. Suzanna and Mr. Ross had come back and were leanin' against the cabin next to the door.

I looked at Tew-yu in her buckskin dress and moccasins and then remembered that I was still in my nightdress. So were Suzanna and Sary.

There were more screams from the cabin. You'd think we'd be used to the screams now, but they got worse and more terrifyin'. These were piercing sounds that hurt just to hear. I squeezed Sary's hand tighter. "It's goin' to be just fine," I said, but for the first time I was doubtin' it myself. Inside me the helpless feelin' was swellin' so that I felt it would soon be chokin' the breath right out of me.

What's a person to do? I swallowed hard, but my

mouth was so dry there was nothin' to swallow. My mind sailed over the feelin' tryin' to see to the other side of it. But I couldn't. I had to be doin' somethin'! A body can't just stand there when a friend needs them! I looked over to Mr. Ross. Sweat ran down his forehead, but he wasn't even wipin' at it, just lettin' it run down his cheeks and into his beard.

Then suddenly, as if my body knew what to do without my mind tellin' it anything, I grabbed the bucket and dipper that was sittin' near the door and ran for the spring. I toted the water back as careful as I could without losin' it on the ground and took the first dipperful to Mr. Ross.

I had to offer three times before I got his attention. Finally he noticed the dipper I was handin' out and took a drink without sayin' a word. He drank the whole thing down and then another, but when I offered a third he shook his head. Next I gave some to Suzanna. She was almost as pale as her ma, but the water seemed to rouse her a mite. Sary and Robert each drank a dipperful.

Next was George, he looked at me strange-like. I couldn't figure why. His face was sweatin' and he looked as parched as anyone else. I shoved the dipper closer. Still he didn't take it but looked to Mr. Ross who of course was payin' him no mind at all.

"Well do ya want some water or don't ya?" I finally asked. He wiped the sweat from his forehead and then lookin' once more at Mr. Ross he took the dipper and drank it down. *Finally*, I thought, but I didn't say it.

Degonda drank up two dippers and so did Lije, but all the rest took just the one. By the time Pa and the little boys had finished there wasn't a drop left.

My mouth was more dry now than ever, what with watchin' them all drinkin'. I was about to fetch another bucket of water when another scream sounded from the cabin and Aunt Hat suddenly was fillin' up the doorway. Her face was pinched and there was blood on her hands. "Millennium, I need you. Come in."

At first I reckoned I'd heard wrong. I was only thirteen! But she had disappeared back inside and Pa was sayin', "You'd better go along. Hat knows best."

I dropped the bucket and walked into the cabin feelin' more terrified than when I'd first gone to the village. The lantern was still burnin' and the heat was suffocatin'. But what I remember most was the feeling of my stomach turning inside of me and my mind drainin' out of my skull so's I could barely think.

"This isn't the way it always is," Aunt Hat said. "Come over here. I need you to help hold her. She's in a lot of pain."

There was blood on the bed and my stomach retched.

"Take a deep breath!" Aunt Hat shouted from some far away place and suddenly I realized she was talkin' to me. "I need you!" I did what she said and the room stopped spinnin' some.

"Come on, Millennium! Just don't think about it. Come over here quick and hold her hands. The baby is coming wrong and I've been trying to get it turned around. Katato's got to help me. *You've* got to tend to Mrs. Ross."

Suddenly Mrs. Ross started groanin' and Aunt Hat began talkin' gentle and soothin'-like. "Just one or two more. That's it. Push hard so I can grab hold of its head." While Aunt Hat strained to turn the baby's head, Katato worked on Mrs. Ross's stomach, pushin' and turnin'. Mrs. Ross screamed and lunged on the bed.

"Hold her down," Aunt Hat yelled at me. "It hurts her, but it's got to be done or we'll lose them both!"

The scream settled into a terrible groanin' and I held her shoulders. "It's goin' to be fine," I found myself sayin'. She took hold of my arm then and almost squeezed it into two pieces. She was breathin' hard and sweat was drenchin' her face. The pain eased up and Aunt Hat told me to wipe her face with the cloth that was on the pillow. I did as I was told without really understandin' what I was doin'. I felt all numb—too numb to even be scared.

"I almost got it that time," Aunt Hat said. "One more good one and I think we can do it. Are you all right, Millennium?" she asked without lookin' at me. "Keep her hands back. Keep her down."

And then the moanin' started all over and Aunt Hat went to work again, and this time I was sure Mrs. Ross was goin' to squeeze my arms right off my body. That pain ended and Mrs. Ross relaxed a mite. I wiped her head again and saw that Katato's and Aunt Hat's foreheads were just as wet. I wiped Katato's. She didn't even look up. Then I wiped Aunt Hat's and as I touched it she looked at me for just a second. "Thank-you," she whispered, and I could tell she was both tired and worried.

But then another pain began and the women were all intent on Mrs. Ross and the baby. Mrs. Ross squeezed my arms and gasped big breaths. I thought sure this time I'd be yellin' too, but just when my arm got to hurtin' so's I couldn't stand it any more, I saw the baby's head and didn't think on my arms any more.

It wasn't at all what I expected. The head was covered with blood and was slimy and wet and more blue than pink. The eyes were closed and I thought certain sure it was dead. My heart took to racin' and I was bitin' on my lip so hard that later I realized I'd drawn blood. Katato stepped back now while Aunt Hat washed off the tiny mouth and nose with a clean cloth. Soon Mrs. Ross began strainin' and pushin' again and this time Aunt Hat pulled and the little body slipped easy-like into her hands. She wiped again at the mouth and nose and then held the baby upside down and slapped her bottom. Suddenly the lifeless form began wiggling and gaspin' for air and cryin'.

"It's a girl," I whispered.

"She's fine," Aunt Hat said, almost laughin'. "She is fit and fine as can be. A mite small, but she is fine!" But she didn't stop workin'. She laid the baby on the bed and quickly tied a piece of twine around the long bloody rope that came out of the baby's stomach, and then she took a knife and cut it. I expected a scream then, but neither the mother nor the baby made a sound. Mrs. Ross lay still, like she was sleepin', and Katato had begun kneading at her stomach as if it was bread dough.

"She's exhausted," Aunt Hat said.

Then the most surprisin' thing happened—Aunt Hat handed me the baby!

"Make her cry again!" she said.

"What?"

"Make her cry! Tip her up again. She's got to get more air into her lungs! Make her cry!" Everything seemed so urgent, her words, the fast way she was workin', the way Katato was workin'.

"She's bleedin' too much," Aunt Hat said, and Katato seemed to understand.

"Make her cry!" Aunt Hat almost screamed at me. It seemed such a cruel thing to do, but I tipped the baby upside down. She didn't make a sound.

"Hit her bottom!" Aunt Hat commanded again. "Make her cry!"

But I couldn't! How can ya hit something that little, something so innocent?

Katato had been tendin' to Mrs. Ross, wipin' her head and sayin' words no one understood, only the sound was gentle and soothin'. But suddenly she reached over Mrs. Ross and hit the baby's bottom. A sound like a scared cat came from the baby and the lips that had been turning blue changed to a red.

"Wrap her in that blanket." Aunt Hat commanded. "Take her out. Keep her warm and if she starts turning blue, make her cry again and if that doesn't help bring her back in."

Once again I couldn't believe what I was hearin'. I was to take care of the baby! I wrapped her up, all the time marvelin' at how tiny she was. Why she wasn't any bigger than the doll Pa had carved for me. Then I walked to the door and opened it.

Mr. Ross was stopped still as winter. Sary raised up her head. And then as if someone told her it was time, the baby suddenly started to squealin' real good. It startled me so's I wasn't sure what to do, but I heard Aunt Hat sayin', "That's a good sound, good sound! Do you hear that?" And I relaxed a bit.

Then the squealin' stopped and the silence was more terrifyin' than the screamin' had been. I knew what Hat meant then. Long as the baby was screamin' I knew she was all right, but now she was quiet I wasn't sure. I looked to see if she was breathin'. She was. I sighed as I started to relax a bit and even felt a mite smart that I was the one holdin' that baby.

Everyone hung in the air like the pictures I'd once seen in a stereo picture machine. It looked so real and yet so not. They hung absolutely still like that for what seemed a millennium, and then I realized they were waitin' on me. Carefully I stepped out and Pa jumped up to shut the door behind me.

The baby wiggled warm in my arms and started whimperin' soft and slow-like, then built up to another healthy cry that sang all the way out to the fields. The sound of new life! Pa called it wailin', but it sounded more like music to me. I'd heard it many times before. I'd heard it comin' through log walls in Winter Quarters. I'd heard it comin' through makeshift canvas tents while crossin' the prairie. I'd even heard it comin' through blankets women were holdin' around a new mother and each time it had sent a warm tickle through me. Only this time, holdin' the baby the way I was, the feelin' was more like lightnin' startin' in my hair and workin' its way to my toenails. I hugged the baby tighter and felt the warmth of that little bein' next to me.

Pa started laughin' first, but it wasn't long till we all were. Sary hugged Suzanna hard and took to dancin'. Even Lije and Jed were jumpin' and hittin' at each other and shoutin'.

"It's a girl!" I said. "Told ya Aunt Hat would do it," I cried, and my insides took to swellin' up with pride.

"Can I see her?" Mr. Ross said, and I held her out for him to get a better look.

As he leaned over I looked into his face and was startled to think that I could ever have thought it a mean face. All I could see was love and a whole mess of joy! Why his face looked beautiful! And suddenly, before I could stop it, tears began floodin' out of my eyes and down my cheeks. It startled me good so that I took to gigglin' too. Mr. Ross took the baby and Sary threw her arms around my neck and she started cryin' and gigglin' along with me.

"Didn't know you had that much water in ya!" Jed teased, but I didn't even care.

With my arms free now, I sat down and just let the tears and the giggles have their way. "We did it!" I cried. "We did it! Everything turned out just fine!" But everyone was carryin' on so, I don't think a soul heard a thing I was sayin'.

CHAPTER 13

$\mathcal{F}$OR THE NEXT HOURS, LIFE AROUND THE CABIN WAS THE most amazin' spectacle I've ever seen. Why it was almost a beehive the way it hummed and buzzed. After Aunt Hat said Mrs. Ross was doing better and Mr. Ross went in to see her, he called for Sary and Suzanna and Robert to come see her. By then the baby was back inside with her mother.

"Land a mighty! Didn't I tell ya Aunt Hat would do it!" I kept sayin' over and over to Sary until finally she said, "I knowed ya told me, Millennium!" but she was still laughin'.

When Mr. Ross came out of the cabin, he shouted for joy—so loud I was sure a body could hear it clean to the top of the mountains. Then he began haulin' things out of his wagons. He gave Katato a sack of sugar and told her to go get the rest of her family.

"No work today!" he said. "We's a-havin' our-
selves a celebratin' feast." He threw out vegetables and
meat and fixin's and began tellin' Suzanna and Sary
what to do. Aromas I'd clean forgot about began fillin'
the air. Sweet taters, salt pork, sweet cakes, and somethin' good made with beans that Sary called Hoppin'
John. She said they had it every New Year's as part of
the celebratin'.

Pa searched the fields until he found enough ripe
corn to add to the feast. Our first corn! Katato came
back with near ten Indians, but she also carried strips
of dried squash, jerked meat, and some real good stuff
called pemmican. Only later did I find out it was made
of ground up dried berries, dried crickets, and animal
fat. Now I'm not so sure it was all that good.

I helped Aunt Hat, Katato, Tew-yu, Sary, and
Suzanna with the cookin' while Lije and Degonda kept
the fires goin'. It's a good thing, too, that Degonda was
there doin' what he kept callin' woman work cause Lije
seemed to be keepin' a better eye on Suzanna than on
the fires. If it weren't for Degonda we might not have
had a fire a'tall. Jed kept eyein' Mr. Ross's wagons and
askin' him what he could do to help. I think he just
wanted a chance to see what all was in those wagons.
What Mr. Ross kept pullin' out was most astonishin'.
And while I didn't keep starin' the way Jed did, I must
be admittin' that those wagons began to seem like they
were possessed with some kind of magic.

"You keep this up," Pa said, "and you won't have anythin' left to sell to the gold miners when you get to California."

"I's got enough," Mr. Ross said as he untied the cradle that had been hangin' beside the wagon. "'Besides, I'm gonna find me some of that gold!"

The Indian men that had come back with Katato sat aways off watchin' every move we made. Why just last week that would have sent the jitters clean through me the way they was starin'. But now I only smiled and sometimes waved and they smiled and waved back. I soon figured that the big one they called Oapitche was Tew-yu's pa. I asked Lije what Oapitche meant. He said, "Big Man."

I smiled and nodded and waved. "Figures!" I said, and Oapitche nodded and waved back.

The fixin' took us hours, but when we finished we had a meal fit for not just a king, but a whole kingdom. Why I'd never in my entire life seen so much food, and my mouth dropped right open when I saw Aunt Hat open her trunk and bring out those blue plates she had been saving for just the right occasion. We ate and ate until I thought my innards would push right through my ribs, but Aunt Hat just kept fillin' those fancy Blue Willow plates so that you couldn't even see that house with wings.

'Fore we knew it, it was evenin' and the sun was sinkin' fast. We were gathered on the shade side of the cabin, and I was restin' against the log wall lookin' up at the soft orange the settin' sun threw over the mountains. It was quiet again—a nice kind of quiet. Only the sound of an occasional fly buzzin' broke into the peace. The men were dozin' against their chests and Aunt Hat and Katato had gone into the cabin to tend to Mrs. Ross, who was still very weak. Sary and Suzanna and Robert were sprawled on a pile of grass that Pa had brought over. What with gettin' up so early they were plumb tuckered. It seemed the only ones not nappin' were me and Mr. Ross.

I looked over to where he was sittin' and was startled to see that he looked as if he was about to cry again. That was a sight hard to imagine let alone behold even though I'd seen it once. I closed my eyes, opened them for another look and certain sure, it was happenin'. Any minute tears would be comin'.

"Everything's all right now, Mr. Ross," I said. "Aunt Hat says Mrs. Ross is doin' right fine. There's no need for worryin' more."

"I ain't worried," Mr. Ross whispered. "I just ain't deservin'."

I wasn't at all sure I knew what he was meanin'. I was too dizzy with food and heat to figure it out. But before I could shut my eyes to join the nappers, Mr. Ross jumped up. He wiped his eyes on his shirt sleeves and commenced shoutin'.

"George, git what I told ya 'bout."

"Yes, sir, Mr. Ross, sir!" George said comin' groggy out of his nap.

I was wide awake now. Pa even turned and stared after George as he trotted to the wagon.

"Fetch yerself out here, Mrs. Boxall," Mr. Ross called to Aunt Hat. Aunt Hat appeared in the doorway.

"Naw! Clean out here!" Mr. Ross said. It was strange how the gruffness hadn't left his voice and yet I wasn't feared of it anymore. I set to wonderin' what had changed—him or me—while Aunt Hat wiped her hands on her apron and stepped out.

"I ain't one fer makin' speeches, but without ya'll my Ginny would never have made it. She told me herself. And fer thankin' ya, Ginny and I want ya'll to have these."

Just then George stepped from 'hind the wagon carryin' a real glass window with four panes!

"There's two of 'em fer ya'll!" Mr. Ross said.

"Why Mr. Ross, I couldn't . . . "

"Cain't argue with me. We's late fer travelin' now, and I's got to get shed a some a this so as to lighten the wagons. Take 'em."

Everyone was stirrin' now. Oapitche grunted and nodded. I didn't think he spoke English, but he sure certain knew what was goin' on. He stood up and motioned for the other Indians to come to him. He said a few words and suddenly they began to dance, makin'

their own music as they did. Degonda jumped up and joined the men.

Tew-yu and Sary came to sit by me while we watched. When the Indians finished, Mr. Ross clapped his hands and shouted.

Suddenly a soft whistlin' sound commenced. It was coming 'round the cabin, but it wasn't really wind. It was melody. Then I saw. It was George playin' on a concertina.

"Oh my!" Sary cried.

"What's the matter?" I asked.

"George ain't played his concertina since Pa sold his ma and pa away. Wouldn't sing neither."

But he was singin' now, and I thought certain sure it was the voice of an angel with the wind itself whistlin' along with him! The sun had disappeared altogether now and everyone sat down to listen. The full moon was shinin' and there were plenty of stars to keep it company. I leaned against the cabin and listened to the sounds, as first happy dancin' kinds of music filled the air, then the slow, sleepy sounds of "Swing Low, Sweet Chariot."

Suddenly I was aware that Aunt Hat was singin'. I hadn't heard Aunt Hat sing since before we'd left Nauvoo. Why, I'd forgotten she could sing so pretty-like. She wasn't singin' the same note as George, but a different one. And then Mr. Ross started in with low notes that were different again, but blendin' with the others so's to make it richer, warmer.

I didn't want to, but I must have fallen asleep. The only other thing I remember was Pa grabbin' me up in his strong arms, snugglin' me against his man-smellin' body like I was somethin' precious, and beddin' me down in the wagon.

CHAPTER 14

*F*OR THE NEXT FEW WEEKS LIFE KEPT ON PERFECT LIKE that. Sary and Robert moved into the wagon with me and Jacob. That made it seem more like we were sisters than just friends. Every time there was a break in the work, Aunt Hat let us go out to the sunflower fields. Sometimes we'd see Tew-yu workin' in the village and she'd wave, and I knew that Sary was wishin' the same thing I was, that Tew-yu, could join us. But she didn't. We went to the village once, however. Tew-yu knew even more English now. She taught us to whistle bird calls that sounded more real than the birds and we taught her to jump rope. Katato didn't like that. She spoke sharply to Tew-yu and even though we couldn't understand the words I knew the meanin'. Tew-yu had work to do and shouldn't be playin'.

Pa and Mr. Ross put the windows in the cabin. They put one on the east so I could see the mountains and one on the north so I could see the village. With windows, even bein' inside wasn't as bad as it had been afore.

Mrs. Ross got to feelin' better even sooner than Aunt Hat said she would. She kept tryin' to help out and Aunt Hat kept scoldin' and tellin' her to sit down. As the color came back into her face, she began to laugh and sing. She had a voice pert near as wonderful as Aunt Hat's, but not quite.

Nights now, after everyone was worked out, we'd all sit outside the cabin and sing and tell stories. Some nights even Tew-yu's family joined us. Those nights were the best. Degonda told wonderful stories about the adventures of the coyote and the wolf. But the very best always came last when George and Aunt Hat led off the music. We'd be singin' the same words, but different notes same as they did the night the baby was born. Aunt Hat called it harmony. Sometimes we'd all join in and the sound would fill up the empty valley until it seemed as if the Millennium had already come.

"Will life be this good evermore?" I asked Aunt Hat on one of those singin' nights under the stars.

"No, Millennium. I wish I could say different, but I can't. There will be more good times, of course. But there will also be bad times. That's just how life is."

"Then I'm goin' to be rememberin' every moment now and keep it for when the bad times come."

Aunt Hat reached around me and in a jerkin' kind of movement hugged me to her. She did that often now, and each time it seemed to feel even better than the last time.

"Like I said before, these last few years haven't been normal. We've had more than our share of the bad times, but we've found a home now that I think we will stay in." She laughed softly and then went on. "Winter's coming and we can start your studies again if you'd like. You were doing so well in Nauvoo."

"I'd like that," I answered.

"Maybe someday you'll even decide to be a midwife."

"Me? Why I almost fainted dead away! I've seen cows and horses born, but I've never seen anythin' like that! I almost lost my breakfast and I hadn't eaten any to be losin'!"

"But what do you remember most now?"

I hadn't thought on that, but as she said it, all I could think about was watchin' that first breath of life fill that lifeless baby. It had been a miracle. Then I remembered, too, the feelin' of holdin' that wigglin', warm baby against my chest and the lightnin' spreadin' through me. "Why I remember the wonder and the joy!" I said.

Aunt Hat laughed. "It's always amazed me how so much pain can bring forth such joy. God must be trying to teach us something, don't you think?"

"Must be," I answered and decided that was something I needed to do a lot more thinkin' on.

"I am so proud of you! Just having new help when I was so tired was a blessing." Aunt Hat hugged me again. "I don't think I could have done it at your age."

She stopped talkin' then and I was glad. All this praisin' was a mite uncomfortable. 'Sides that, George was playin' the concertina now, and I wanted to listen.

"What's the name of this here place anyways?" Mr. Ross interrupted my thinkin'.

"Just east and south is Sessions Settlement. But we're far enough away I'm hopin' this can be a place of its own," Pa said.

"So what ya'll callin' it?"

"Heritage. Finally I've found me a home I think I'll be keepin', a place for my children and theirs and on maybe until the Millennium. It might be a desert now, but it's goin' to blossom like a rose."

"I'd say that's a fine heritage," Mr. Ross said.

"Yep," Pa replied. "A desert that's been turned into a garden by one row of water at a time!"

"Speakin' on names, Mrs. Ross and I's settled on one fer the babe," Mr. Ross said.

"What is it?" Aunt Hat asked.

"We's namin' her Millennium."

I thought my skin would slip right off my bones!

"Sary said she'd call her that no matter what name we put to 'er. But it was fittin'. We's a-fixin' on a new life, and from what I hears, California could use a reminder of the Millennium, too."

Sary looked at me. By the moonlight I could see her smilin' and twistin' at her hair. I smiled back thinkin', on how every moment just kept gettin' better. But then Mr. Ross said, "We's goin' soon. Ginny says she's up to travelin'. I'll make her and the babe cozy as I can in the wagon. If we don't go soon we won't make the mountain pass before the snows."

"It might be too late already," Pa said slowly.

"Then we'll just go west as far as we can and wait out the winter. But I've got to be movin' on."

He went on talkin' with Pa, but I didn't hear. Suddenly the high as the moon feelin' I'd been taken with fell crashin' into the lowest of valleys. Havin' a friend had been everything I'd dreamed it would be and more. We'd worked side by side, giggled in the wagon when we should have been sleepin', made corn husk dolls together, woven dandelions into crowns, and waded in the creek. Why we'd even talked on how it would be when we were married and had babies of our own. Sary had read *Last of the Mohicans* and loved it same as me. (I told Jed it wasn't just a book for boys!) Sary said she cried real tears when Cora died, but I read it in the days before I knew how to cry.

Now she'd be goin' and I'd be left alone with five brothers. The thought made tears spring into my eyes.

"It's all right," Aunt Hat said, wipin' away the tears with her apron. "You've got the memories."

"How did you know what I was thinkin'?"

"I've been lonely before, too."

I'd never thought about Aunt Hat bein' lonely, but then I realized she was the only white woman for miles around. She hugged me again. It was still a stiff Aunt Hat kind of hug, but I knew her heart was in it. "They'll be more time now. Maybe even better times. I'll teach you quiltin' and needlework."

How could there be better times without Sary? I wondered. Sary promised she'd send me letters and I could write to her anytime I wanted, but it wouldn't be the same.

The tears wouldn't stop but they slowed down a mite, and I leaned on Aunt Hat's arm and let my whole heart listen to the music comin' out of George's hands and mouth. He was singin' the Mormon pioneer song Aunt Hat had taught him, and everyone began joinin' in. I listened to the words, and memories came to mind of the many awful, hurtin' times when I sung it 'round a campfire somewheres on the prairie. It'd been a whisper of hope then. Now it was alive with peace.

They finished all four verses, and Mrs. Ross, cuddlin' little Millennium, said, "Please sing it again." And so we did.

Come, come, ye Saints, no toil nor labor fear;
But with joy wend your way.
Though hard to you this journey may appear.
Grace shall be as your day.
'Tis better far for us to strive
Our useless cares from us to drive;
Do this, and joy your hearts will swell—
All is well! All is well!

I decided right then that every time I looked through one of those windows Mr. Ross had given us, I was goin' to see Sary on the other side. Every time I looked at a star, I was goin' to hear George singin'. And every time I heard the squeal of a new born baby, I was goin' to think about the Millennium, the one Isaiah talked on.

I joined in the singin' again. We finished the last "All is well!" and no one moved.

"It's a beautiful song," Sary whispered.

"It is," I said.

"I'll always remember you, Millennium," Sary said.

"And I'll always remember you, Sary girl!"

Aunt Hat started the song once more. Her voice was so close that it filled me not just with sound but with quivers. Somewhere in the third verse I finally joined in. "We'll make the air with music ring, Shout praises to our God and King; Above the rest these words we'll tell—All is well! All is well!"

I couldn't sing more. Aunt Hat patted my arm in that way a mother has of sayin' "I love you," and in that moment I knew that even though Sary was leavin', somehow everything would be all right. I sat back and watched the stars and let the music fill me up.

$\mathcal{A}$BOUT THE $\mathcal{A}$UTHOR

Sherrie Johnson spent her growing up years in an orchard, a hollow, and on a mountain—the hollow in Brigham City, Utah, the mountain and orchard in Centerville, Utah. She now lives in West

Photo by: Jim Child

Bountiful (still in Utah), on what was once an Indian watering hole, with her husband Carl and six of her ten children. The oldest daughters have added their husbands and five grandsons to the family.

Sherrie loves to read—even though she's too big to do it in cherry trees any more—and of course write. She has written over 100 short stories and articles since 1970 and is the author of twelve other published books.

Besides Utah, Sherrie has lived in Texas and Germany and has visited places like Egypt, Israel, and Greece. However, the strings attached to her heart always bring her home to Utah.

When she isn't writing, studying, or doing things with her family, Sherrie loves to swim and play racquetball.